Crackadillo

GARY LEE VINCENT

Crackadillo
By **Gary Lee Vincent**

Burning Bulb Publishing
P.O. Box 4721
Bridgeport, WV 26330-4721
United States of America
www.BurningBulbPublishing.com

Cover designed by Max Cave as a work for hire for Gary Lee Vincent and Burning Bulb Publishing.

First Edition.

Paperback Edition ISBN: 978-1-964172-12-5

Also by Gary Lee Vincent

Novels
PASSAGEWAY
BELLY TIMBER
ATTACK OF THE MELONHEADS
WHEN THE BEDPOSTS SHAKE (RING OF THE SUCCUBUS)
IMPOUND
STRANGE FRIENDS
THE BEST ACTORS THAT EVER LIVED
JEROME
THE BLIND MELODY

Darkened—The West Virginia Vampire Series
DARKENED HILLS
DARKENED HOLLOWS
DARKENED WATERS
DARKENED SOULS
DARKENED MINDS
DARKENED DESTINIES

The Douglas River Vampire Series
RIVER: A VAMPIRE'S NIGHTMARE
ICARUS

The Crackimals Series
CRACKCOON
CRACKODILE
CRACKSQUATCH
CRACKROACHES
CRACKADILLO

The Black Circle Chronicles
PROVE YOUR LOVE
STRANGE NEW POWERS
NIGHT WINGS
SHEEP AMONGST WOLVES
LORD OF THE BIRDS

Nonfiction
THE WINNER, THE LOSER
AGELATIONS
CONFIGURATION MANAGEMENT

Musical Releases
100 PERCENT
PASSION, PLEASURE, & PAIN
SOMEWHERE DOWN THE ROAD

Dedicated to
Solon Tsangaras

CHAPTER 1

It was after his older brother Slim shot the armadillo that Cody Mitchell agreed he and his family needed a vacation up north.

But that's getting ahead of the story.

***

Young Jimmy Mitchell stood on the rear porch of his dad's ranch house in Destin, Texas, and stared out at the cows eating in the pasture back there. Uncle Slim rode past the house on a tall, dark horse and waved at him.

Jimmy waved back at Uncle Slim.

Jimmy was eight years old and Uncle Slim scared him a little. Not in a creepy child-molesting sort of way, but because Uncle Slim seemed rather random in his behavior. Most times he was okay, but sometimes he'd just snap and act all crazy like.

***

As was usual most days after school, that afternoon Tommy Lee came visiting and soon he and Jimmy Mitchell were shooting at each other on the X-Box.

Tommy Lee was the son of one of the ranch hands and Jimmy's best friend. After they'd played Fortnite for a while, Tommy Lee seemed to remember something. "Hey, where you gonna hide Rocky this time?" the little boy asked.

"Huh? What you talkin' 'bout?" Jimmy asked back.

Tommy Lee explained: "I heard on the news that the animal controllers are gonna be killing armadillos again."

"What!?" Jimmy felt like someone had poured cold water on him. "Again?" In his young mind the image of the 'animal controllers' loomed large and terrible.

Jimmy's class teacher, Miss Hodge, had recently taught them about the Nazis—a group of bad people who'd locked people up during the Second World War—and that was exactly how Jimmy viewed the state of Texas's Animal Control Department—as jackbooted thugs who captured animals and 'concentrated' them in camps where they did all kinds of terrible things to them.

"Where am I gonna hide Rocky?" he almost wailed. All this while they'd still been playing the video game and now Tommy Lee shot down two of Jimmy's onscreen soldiers.

"Hey, that's cheating. I wasn't concentrating." Then, because it occurred to him that Tommy Lee might just be lying to scare him and gain an advantage in their video game, Jimmy looked shrewdly at Tommy Lee. "Are you sure about this? I mean about the animal controllers?"

This time Tommy Lee paused the game before replying. "Yes. It was on the news this morning. They say the 'dillos have lep . . . lepro . . . I don't remember the name now."

"Leprosy," Jimmy filled in for him in a scared voice.

"Yeah, the 'dillos all have leprosy, which is bad for people. And so, the animal controllers are gonna catch 'em all and . . . do something bad to 'em. What's leprosy anyway?"

Jimmy tried to remember what his father had told him about it. "It's this sickness that makes your fingers all fall off and your nose too."

Tommy Lee's eyes widened in fright. "Do you think Rocky has leprosy?"

"I . . . I dunno."

Both young boys abandoned their game and headed out back to Rocky's pen.

Rocky was young Jimmy Mitchell's 'pet' nine-band armadillo. Some months ago they'd found the armadillo wandering around near the house and one of the ranch hands had caught it. He'd been about cooking it, when Jimmy had pleaded for its life, saying he wanted it for a pet.

According to Jimmy's dad, it was illegal to have an armadillo as a pet in their state of Texas, so neither Jimmy nor Tommy Lee could tell anyone about Rocky being here. But Jimmy's dad and Uncle Slim had filled up the old kid's swimming pool and then fenced it around and put Rocky in there.

The way they'd done it, there was concrete and chain-linked steel mesh underground that the armadillo couldn't dig through and it couldn't escape overground either, because the enclosure was also fenced around with chain-linked wire. Rocky didn't seem to want to leave anyway. Jimmy and the family threw the armadillo food scraps every day, usually whatever was left from dinner.

Now the two little boys stared at the 'pet' armadillo's enclosure, which was shaded by a huge tree, and also contained two pet rabbits. They looked around for Rocky, but he was underground.

Tommy Lee turned to Jimmy. "Let's go finish the game."

Jimmy nodded. "I'll ask dad about the animal controllers later."

So, they returned to their X-Box war games.

CHAPTER 2

That evening, Jimmy did ask his dad about the animal controllers.

Jimmy's father Cody was tall and tending toward fat, with dark hair and sunburned skin from long hours spent up in the saddle tending to his cows. He had a mustache but no beard, gray eyes, and lots of wrinkles.

"I haven't heard anything about that yet," he told Jimmy. Then he looked across the dinner table at his girlfriend Wendy. "Hon, you heard any news 'bout a 'dillo leprosy outbreak recently?"

Wendy Hearst was a little younger than Cody, a tall and shapely brunette. (Jimmy's mother had died some years ago, and Cody still felt the loss of her passing. Wendy was doing her very best to comfort Cody, and was mostly succeeding.)

Wendy shook her head. "No, I don't . . ." Then she remembered something and nodded. "Yeah, sweetie, one of the girls at the salon mentioned something like that yesterday. I wasn't paying much attention tho'."

"Hmmm," Cody Mitchell said, scratching his chin. "Hmmm."

To Jimmy, his father's lack of comment other than 'hmmm' confirmed his worst fears. So yes, Tommy Lee had been telling him the truth.

"What we gonna do 'bout Rocky, daddy?" Jimmy asked in a worried voice.

His dad smiled at him. "Now, son, don't you start worrying yourself about that little 'dillo of yours. No one's gonna ever know he's out there. They'll think it's just the two rabbits living in the enclosure."

Jimmy nodded, but looked unconvinced. "Dad, does Rocky have leprosy?"

Wendy laughed. "Whatever gave you that idea?"

Cody smiled benevolently at his son. "No, boy, your little friend don't have leprosy. He's been here for months, and hasn't had contact with any other 'dillos in all that time."

Jimmy nodded. He was still worried though.

"You look deathly tired, sweetie," Wendy told Jimmy's father, changing the subject. "Are you feeling alright?"

Cody Mitchell shook his head. "Not really. All this ranching is giving me ulcers, what with the recent fluctuating prices of beef exports."

Wendy nodded sympathetically. "Sweetie, what you need is a nice long vacation."

"I haven't had a vacation in years; part of the trouble with being one's own boss. I wish I had an employer who'd insist on me taking some time off." He chewed some steak and then sighed. "Taking a few days off of work is easy enough. The trouble is if I hang around here I tend to naturally think of the ranch work, and then I cut short my vacation 'cos there's so much to do."

"Maybe we should travel."

Cody Mitchell nodded. "Hmm, hon, maybe you're right. But where can we go?"

Wendy drank some water, then said. "How 'bout if we travel northeast to West Virginia?"

"Never been there before. What's to do there?"

"Nothing much, which is the whole idea. That far away from the ranch there's no danger of you suddenly rushing home 'cos two cows fell sick."

Cody Mitchell nodded. "Hmmm, sounds good, honey. I'm sure Slim can run things for a couple weeks without me."

Wendy laughed. "It won't be a disaster. Everyone already knows their jobs. He just has to oversee things; make sure they don't slack off when you ain't here." Wendy put down her fork and picked up the phone. "I've a cousin in Buckhannon WV. Charlotte Bentley. If we do decide to head out there for a few days, she'll help us make accommodation arrangements. Or better yet, Charlotte's husband is a park ranger. We can spend the time camping."

"Hmmm," Cody Mitchell said. "Sounds good."

Jimmy ate his food in silence. Listening to his parents was depressing him. Neither his dad nor Wendy were taking things as seriously as he thought they should. Rocky's terrible danger seemed almost a joke to them.

Jimmy's young mind began making backup plans.

***

The next day, after school, Jimmy's worst fears seemed to have been realized. Though he and Tommy Lee arrived from school together, as usual, they split up once through the house gate, with Tommy Lee heading over to his father's cabin, while Jimmy kept on straight ahead to the main ranch house.

When Jimmy walked up the driveway to the front door, he saw a police car parked outside the ranch house and his father talking to two men—one white, one black—with equally cold expressions on their faces.

Jimmy greeted his father and the two men and hurried into the house. *Damn, it's them! It's the animal controllers!*

As fast as he could, he ditched his school bag and ran out looking for Tommy Lee. (Jimmy, of course, had no idea that the two men his father was talking to were policemen looking for a runaway murder suspect, thought to be hiding in this area.)

Once Tommy Lee heard Jimmy's news, the two boys hurried back over to the house and peeked around the side of the building at the two men.

"Yeah, it's def'nit'ly the animal controllers," Tommy Lee agreed.

"What we gonna do, Tommy? They'll find Rocky for sure, once they start looking."

Tommy Lee shook his head. "Not if we hide him first."

To their relief, the 'animal controllers' soon departed, without the pet armadillo.

***

That night, after Jimmy's father and Wendy had gone to bed, operation 'Protect Rocky' was launched.

Once certain the coast was clear, Jimmy sneaked out of the ranch house and hurried over to Tommy Lee's house again. After gently rapping on Tommy Lee's bedroom window for a while, he waited till the other boy showed up outside.

Then, they both made their quiet way over to Rocky's enclosure.

"You got the bacon?" Tommy Lee asked Jimmy.

Jimmy produced a strip of uncooked bacon from his pajama pocket. "Got it right here."

Once at the armadillo enclosure, Jimmy unlocked the gate and stepped inside, while Tommy Lee kept watch in case their parents started looking for them.

Both of the rabbits were fast asleep in their hutches. One of them even appeared to be snoring, its little nose twitching with each breath.

"Hey, Rocky, come on out!" Jimmy whispered, going in turn to each of the armadillo's three holes and repeating himself while wagging the strip of bacon at the hole entrance.

On the second attempt at the second hole, Rocky poked his head out of the hole. Then, sniffing the air cautiously, the armadillo emerged fully.

"Good boy," Jimmy whispered and picked Rocky up. The armadillo made no attempt to escape his grasp. It was used to his smell, and besides, it wanted the bacon he'd brought it.

"Let's go!" Tommy Lee said.

With the armadillo in his arms, Jimmy hurried outside the enclosure, and Tommy Lee locked it behind him.

Then, standing there with the moon beaming down on them, Tommy Lee asked: "But, Jimmy, where do we put him so the animal controllers can't find him?"

Jimmy had already figured that out. "We'll hide him in Uncle Slim's cabin," he said, producing the spare key Uncle Slim left permanently in the ranch house from the pajama pocket that didn't have bacon in it. "He and Cousin Lisa have gone to Dallas. Dad says they won't be back home for days." He nodded. "We can leave Rocky in Uncle Slim's cabin for two days, and put him back in the enclosure if the animal controllers don't come back here by Friday."

"Two days is good," Tommy Lee agreed.

So that's what the two little boys did. They snuck Rocky into Uncle Slim's cabin, which was the closest one to the house, left food (lots of bacon) and water for the armadillo, and then each went home and climbed into bed feeling very satisfied that Operation 'Protect Rocky' had been a success.

CHAPTER 3

For two days afterward, everything went fine. With Slim Mitchell away from home, Jimmy and Tommy Lee realized their plan had succeeded, particularly when the two 'animal controllers' returned the next day to ask Jimmy's dad some questions and then once more left without taking Rocky with them.

"Okay, we'll return Rocky to his home tomorrow night," Tommy Lee said when he and Jimmy met up to feed the armadillo that afternoon.

Jimmy nodded and set down some chunks of cheese and a saucerful of milk for Rocky.

"Hey, is your uncle's cabin always in such a mess?" Tommy Lee asked. "This place looks really torn up."

Jimmy suddenly looked worried. "Hey, you don't think Rocky tore the carpet up like this?" he asked. "Uncle Slim's gonna be mad if he did."

"What we'll do," Tommy Lee said, with eight-year-old wisdom, "is not tell Uncle Slim we came in here. Then he'll blame someone else."

Jimmy agreed that this plan would work. "Yeah, that's good. Hey, Rocky, Rocky, come out and eat."

The armadillo didn't show, but they soon found it fast asleep under Uncle Slim's couch, which now looked a lot more shredded than Jimmy remembered. The same went for the rug, the window drapes, and lots of other furniture.

***

The problem was that Slim Mitchell came back before they could return Rocky.

9

Tommy Lee and Jimmy arrived back from school the next afternoon and there was Uncle Slim's battered pickup truck in the driveway, and there was Jimmy's older cousin Lisa alighting from the pickup truck.

"Oops, I think we're in trouble," Tommy Lee said.

"We'll just do like you said, act like we didn't do nothing," Jimmy said.

"Ouch, my backside already hurts from the tanning it'll git if my dad ever hears about this."

Instead of splitting up like they usually did on their way home from school, today the two boys stayed together. Together, they watched Cousin Lisa wave to Cody's father and then walk around the side of the house towards her and her dad's cabin.

They hurried after Lisa Mitchell to see what was going to happen. They watched Lisa open the door of the cabin and step inside. Then a few seconds later Lisa stepped back outside of the cabin and screamed.

"Daddy!" she yelled. "Daddy, come here quickly!"

A few seconds later, Slim Mitchell came running over, wondering what the commotion was all about.

"There's an armadillo in the house! It ripped everything up!"

Slim looked shocked. Then he, too, stepped inside the cabin. "Dammit, the little sonofabitch even crapped in my shoes!" There was silence from the cabin, then Uncle Slim yelled, "Come here, you li'l sonofabitch! "Come back here! Lisa, shut the door!"

But Lisa wasn't fast enough. She did get the cabin door shut, but not before Rocky had slipped out past her. The armadillo stood there looking confused for a moment, then set off running towards his enclosure.

Tommy Lee shoved Jimmy in the back. "Go fetch your dad quick, or else Rocky's dead meat. Uncle Slim might roast and eat him."

Jimmy nodded and ran for the ranch house. "Dad, day, come quick. Uncle Slim's gonna kill Rocky!"

***

Summoned by the commotion, Cody Mitchell was already exiting the rear of the ranch house, when Jimmy arrived to call him.

"What the hell's goin' on out here, boy?" he demanded of Jimmy, grabbing him by the shoulders and shaking him.

Jimmy pointed at Slim, who was advancing towards them with a revolver in his hand. "He wants to kill Rocky."

Cody Mitchell looked at his older brother and saw that Slim was incensed. "Hey Slim, calm down. Don't you do nothing rash now!"

But Slim Mitchell brushed him aside. "You stay out of it. This is between me and that terrorist 'dillo."

The 'terrorist armadillo' was, in the meantime, confused. Rocky was running in circles around his enclosure, scratching at the chain-link fence, and wondering why in the hell he couldn't get into that place of assured safety.

Meanwhile, the two rabbits in the enclosure were staring at him like they'd like to help him out, but they didn't know how to unlock the gate either.

"C'mon, Slim, calm yourself down!" Cody pleaded again. He didn't dare go near Slim when the man was holding a gun. Nor did anyone else, for that matter. The ranch hands who'd been alerted by the commotion were also keeping a safe distance from Slim.

"I'm gonna kill you, you damn terrorist anteater!" Slim thundered. "How dare you poop in my shoes?"

"Yeah, kill it, Daddy!" Lisa yelled, "It tore my dresses up too!"

Slim fired at Rocky. The bullet zinged past the armadillo by a hair's breadth and burrowed into the sand.

The noise threw Rocky into an additional panic. But, seemingly constrained from running away by force of habit, he continued trying to enter his enclosure. The two rabbits had meanwhile made themselves scarce in their hutches.

"Dammit, Rocky is dead for sure," Tommy Lee told Jimmy.

"This is our fault," Jimmy wept.

"No, it's the fault of the animal controllers," Tommy Lee told him. "They're like those Nazis Miss Hodges told us about."

"You're right," Jimmy agreed.

Uncle Slim fired again, and then when that bullet missed also, he stepped up close to the armadillo, took slow and careful aim, and pulled the trigger.

This time Slim didn't miss. But the result wasn't what anyone had expected. Yes, there was the expected gunshot noise, but right after that everyone heard a sort of 'zinging' noise also, and after that Slim Mitchell fell backwards holding his belly and howling in pain.

"The damn 'dillo shot me!" Slim howled. "The damn critter shot me!"

"Daddy!" Lisa screamed and hurried over to his side.

Everybody at the rear of the house also now ran over to Slim's side.

It was a crazy situation. While Rocky the armadillo seemed none the worse for wear, the man who'd wanted to kill him was now bleeding from a bullet wound to the gut.

Slim had dropped his gun when he'd fallen down. Jimmy's father quickly picked the gun up, and stuck it in his back pocket. He tried not to laugh, while saying: "Hey, someone call a darn ambulance. Tell them Slim got hit by a ricochet while trying to kill an armadillo."

"I'm gonna kill that damn terrorist," Slim mumbled and then fainted.

Jimmy and Tommy Lee let Rocky back into his enclosure, where, as if he was shell-shocked, the armadillo waddled over to the nearest burrow hole and vanished.

Once Rocky was out of sight, both boys heaved loud sighs of relief.

Then they both noticed Cousin Lisa staring at them. "I just know the both of you had something to do with this," she said with a nasty look in her eyes.

"Honest, it wasn't us," Jimmy protested, while he and Tommy Lee did their best to look as innocent as possible.

Wendy had been asleep and had missed all the action. She'd even slept through the noise of all three gunshots. But the sound of the ambulance arriving roused her.

"What the hell happened?" Wendy asked when she'd joined everyone else.

Cody told her about Slim's plan to kill Rocky backfiring on him. Wendy tried not to laugh as the paramedics wheeled Slim, who was awake again but looking dazed, over to their ambulance.

"You know, hon," Cody Mitchell told Wendy as the ambulance drove off, "I think it's time for you to call up your cousin Charlotte and let her know we'll be visiting." He nodded. "Yeah, we'd better go on that damn vacation to West Virginia, before I go as crazy as Slim."

CHAPTER 4

Slim Mitchell was out of the hospital four days later. He'd been very fortunate; the deflected bullet had just missed nicking his stomach, which would have required major surgery. As it was, the wound was mostly through muscle, and the bullet had easily been removed.

Once Slim was home again, the plans for the family trip to WV began in earnest. The looming midterm break meant Jimmy would be off school for a while so everything seemed to be falling into place. As there was really no way Slim could oversee the ranch in his current condition, he'd be coming along too, which meant Lisa would also be coming along to look after him.

Jimmy viewed Uncle Slim's accompanying them with mixed feelings.

This was because his father had agreed to let him bring Rocky along also.

"What!" had been Slim's comment when he'd heard that the 'terrorist 'dillo' would be going cross-country with the family.

Jimmy's father had then pulled him aside and whispered in his ear that he'd had no choice, that Jimmy was still scared stiff that the animal would be caught and put in a leper colony, and he didn't want the headache of the kid pestering him all the time they were in West Virginia over whether "the 'dillo was still free."

That piece of info cracked up even Slim Mitchell. "A leper colony, huh? What the hell they teach kids in school nowadays?"

"The Nazi animal controllers are gonna concentrate the 'dillos in a leper colony," was what Tommy Lee had misinformed Jimmy.

Rocky would be coming along, too. Cody Mitchell bought the armadillo a cage and borrowed a special leash so the animal wouldn't dig himself a burrow where they couldn't find him.

The day of departure arrived. The family packed themselves and their luggage into their rented Class B camper, loaded Rocky in also, jauntily perched their ten-gallon hats on their heads, and then hit the road heading north.

None of them had the slightest idea that they were traveling towards disaster.

CHAPTER 5

"So, they'll be arriving tomorrow?" park ranger Gary Bentley asked his wife Charlotte as they sat having dinner in their home in Buckhannon, West Virginia.

Charlotte looked up from reading emails on her cellphone. "Uh huh. Wendy expects they'll be here by mid-afternoon."

Gary swallowed his mouthful of food, then said. "It's too bad we don't have enough space here to accommodate five people."

Charlotte laughed. "Oh, don't worry about that, darling. Wendy assures me it's no trouble at all. She says they really do want to camp out in the open. Otherwise, they'd have simply booked a motel for their stay here."

Gary nodded. "Yeah, but what about the kid? And his uncle, the one who shot the armadillo and . . . ?" Gary began laughing now. "I guess turnabout really is fair play."

Charlotte, an animal lover, scowled. "I actually think it served Slim right. Why shoot at the poor animal in the first place?"

Gary continued laughing. "Well, honey, you did say it destroyed the guy's furniture . . . and shit in his best pair of shoes. If I was judging the case in a court of law, I'd definitely consider that as 'provocation' or 'just cause.'"

" 'Provocation' or 'just cause' indeed." But Charlotte now began laughing, too.

CHAPTER 6

Later that night, a short while after park ranger Gary Bentley got through helping his wife load up their dishwasher, and in the same town of Buckhannon, WV, a young hoodlum named Toby Miller and his equally delinquent girlfriend Alice Brown were cautiously observing the home of a local drug dealer named Eddie Bush from a point across the road from his front driveway.

"How soon are we gonna do this?" Alice asked Toby. "I'm beginning to get the shakes again."

"Calm down and lower your damn voice!" Toby harshly whispered to her.

"I can't help it," she whispered back in an urgent voice. "You know how bad it gets, baby!"

"Yes, yes, I do. I'm feeling just as bad. But please, girl, try to get a fucking hold of yourself. If Eddie so much as suspects that we're out here, we're both dead meat."

"Okay, okay. You're yelling too now!"

Realizing that she was right, Toby lowered his voice, then turned away from Alice and resumed watching Eddie Bush's place from behind their chosen tree.

The reason for this stakeout was simple: Toby had received a tip-off from a friend of his who worked for Eddie Bush. The friend had told him that Eddie had a large stash of Agent Orange hidden in his house.

Now, both Toby and Alice were hardcore druggies. You name it, they'd done it. But now, they were both hooked on Agent Orange, the newest drug in town and, according to the feds, possibly the most habit-forming narcotic in existence. Both Toby and Alice already had the orange-tinted eyes that marked some 'orange' users in the later stages of addiction, and both also regularly exhibited the associated violent urges, which was simply another reason that US law enforcement was doing their absolute best to stamp out Agent Orange usage.

Their friend Carlos simply wanted cash from the sale of the drug, but Toby and Alice wanted the drug for themselves.

"Why the hell won't this sonofabitch leave home for his damn party?" Toby suddenly grunted aloud, forgetting that he'd just cautioned his girlfriend against similarly raising her voice.

Alice hissed at him but said nothing. Toby was in withdrawal himself; if she gave him any lip, he might backhand her or worse. So, she held her tongue, though she felt like cussing him stupid, or even stabbing him with the knife in her purse. That was how bad the drug cravings were on her. She concentrated as best she could on their target, the small house opposite them, where that whole lot of Agent Orange was waiting for them to steal it.

"Okay, baby, here they come now!" Toby suddenly whispered.

Across the street, Eddie Bush was coming out of his front door. A small, wiry, middle-aged man who looked more like a gymnastics teacher than one of West Virginia's top drug dealers, he was accompanied by his wife Wanda and a huge bodyguard, whose name neither Toby nor Alice knew.

The bodyguard opened the back door of the black Mercedes for Wanda and Eddie and then got in the driver's seat.

A minute later, the Mercedes backed out into the street and headed west. The coast was now clear for Toby and Alice.

"Can we move now?" Alice asked once the black vehicle had turned off the street. "I feel like ants are walking over me."

"Not yet, baby," Toby cautioned. "Let's wait another two minutes. In case they forget something and come back for it."

Those two minutes felt like an hour to both of them. But finally, Toby decided that all was fine, and they dashed across the road to the side entrance of Eddie's house.

Toby's friend Carlos was waiting for them at the side entrance. "Okay, let's do this," he said. "Shit, bro, I thought the boss would never leave for his party. Wanda was almost going nuts at the thought that they'd be missing all of the fun."

"What the hell kept him in so late?" Toby asked.

Carlos gestured to them to follow him. "Some guy who works in a circus wants to buy Agent Orange. Which sucks for us, 'cos it means we can't steal all of it like I'd intended." He looked back at the others as they accompanied him through the house. "As far as I could tell, until that circus guy called, the boss had completely forgotten he's even got this stash here. You know how the feds have been breathing super-hot down his neck for ages 'cos they suspect he sold the orange to that high school kid who murdered his parents? So, the way I figured it, Eddie Bush wasn't gonna remember the orange until that blew over, which might've been a year from now."

They'd reached a small back room, a study with three large bookcases.

"This place looks completely legit," Alice said.

"Yeah, it looks like a lawyer's office," Toby agreed with her.

"Don't be fooled," Carlos said. "Some of the books are fakes."

He knelt down and pulled out one of the encyclopedias at the bottom of the closest bookcase and opened it up. The book was completely hollow inside, with its interior filled with several packages of orange candy.

"Wow!" Toby exclaimed on seeing how much Agent Orange the hollow book contained, and it was a whole lot.

"See?" Carlos asked with a smile. "Eddie Bush actually brought the feds in here when they came to interview him. The suckers didn't suspect a thing."

"This is so cool," Alice said in an awed voice. "Can we . . . can I . . . ?"

"Sure, go ahead," Carlos said, flinging her one of the packages. "There's plenty to go around. "Now that this carnival guy—from what I overhead, the dude trains a boxing kangaroo—anyway, now that the guy's in town, Eddie's gonna need about a third of his stash for the guy, but the rest is more than enough to put us all in the money for a while."

Alice had already popped an orange 'marshmallow' between her lips and was chewing delightedly on it. That was one of the benefits of Agent Orange—you didn't actually need a crack pipe to smoke it. Sure, eating it halved the high you got (some users claimed it cut the high down by two-thirds), but the benefits of being able to orally ingest the drug compensated for this. If you were somewhere where there were lots of people, for instance, even cops, you could just pop the orange 'candies' into your mouth, and no one would be the wiser.

"You know, I never really understood the thrill you guys get from doing this shit," Carlos said with a little shudder when he saw Toby also popping several chunks of Agent Orange into his mouth and chewing them. "It even makes your eyes go weird after a while. But then, crack cocaine never really worked for me, possibly because I saw the harm it caused in the ghetto I grew up in in the Big Apple. I recall my cousin Salvador getting high on crack and blowing his own brains out—that suicide trip of his did it for me. Since then, all I ever mess with is weed and occasionally coke. Anything else is too heavy for me."

Alice and Toby nodded like they understood, and Carlos went on:

"Alright, guys, now, here's what we're gonna do. I'm gonna separate the drugs into two packages, and you guys are gonna leave with one of 'em. I'll make up the difference with packs of regular coke, so that when Eddie does look in on it, he'll think that was all there was in the first place. What you think 'bout that?"

Toby shook his head. "Hey, man, how 'bout if we just kill you and take everything? That way, Eddie's gonna know he's been robbed, but he won't know who did it."

"Yeah, that sounds like a great plan," Alice agreed, pulling her switchblade out of her purse and snapping it open. "Whatcha think, Carlos? How 'bout we kill you and just take everything?"

Carlos sighed. "Stop joking, guys. What I'm proposing is the right way to handle this. Sure, Eddie keeps a close watch on things…"

"We aren't joking, man," Toby said, grabbing Carlos by his hair. The sight of all that glorious Agent Orange, now theirs for the taking, had completely screwed up his sense of right and wrong.

Before Carlos could even protest, Toby had clamped a hand over his mouth to prevent him from talking, and then he nodded to Alice. "Do it, baby!"

Alice ran forward and stabbed Carlos in the throat. She dug the knife deep into the man's neck while he gurgled and swayed but didn't fall over because Toby still had a handful of his hair. Just like her boyfriend was doing, Alice made a point of keeping out of the way of the red arterial spray when she pulled the switchblade out after slitting Carlos's throat from ear to ear.

Then Toby pushed Carlos's body down to the rug, where he quickly bled to death.

"Wow, baby, all the orange is ours now!" Toby said while Alice wiped her knife clean on Carlos's hair.

"Yeah," she agreed. "But we need to hide for a while. The pigs will soon be searching for us."

Toby knelt down and began picking up the packages of Agent Orange that had spilled from the book Carlos had been holding. He quickly transferred the drugs to a plastic bag he'd had in the back pocket of his jeans. He left out the pack he and Alice were already using.

"You know," he told his girlfriend while he worked. "I don't think Eddie Bush is really gonna bother calling the cops on this. Seeing as, according to Carlos, they're already sweating him over that high school kid's death, he won't want the additional attention." Toby nodded down at their murdered friend. "So, I suspect Carlos here will simply find himself occupying a grave somewhere out in the mountains, where Eddie usually disposes of folks who've ripped him off. And after that, Carlos will officially become listed as 'missing.' "

"Yeah, yeah, true," Alice agreed, reaching for another chunk of Agent Orange.

Then Toby said. "But still, baby, I agree with you. I see no reason why we shouldn't be cautious. We should lie low for a few days, till the heat of Carlos's death blows over."

Alice nodded. "Yeah, Toby, but where we gonna hide where no one's gonna think of looking for us?"

Eddie laughed. "Easy, baby. Let's go camping."

CHAPTER 7

The visitors had arrived, and Gary Bentley was trying to make sense of the temporary state of chaos in his house.

To his mind, there simply wasn't enough space in the building for five additional people, not counting the kid's pet armadillo.

Or rather, there *was* enough space for everyone, but Gary wasn't used to having his house this full of people. It reminded him of Christmas when he'd been little, and all of the family relatives would jam themselves in his granddad's little cottage like sardines in a can. He'd never really gotten used to that level of bustle.

Which was possibly another reason why he'd grown up to be a park ranger. Sure, it was a family tradition that had passed down from grandfather to father to son, but maybe the root of that tradition lay in a genetic disposition toward seeking peace and quiet. And the woods certainly provided peace and quiet in spades.

Anyway, Gary Bentley did his best to enjoy his new full house and soon discovered the experience to be far from painful.

Amusingly, the visitors had arrived wearing ten-gallon hats that clearly marked them as being from a ranching state.

He got on famously with Cody Mitchell, and, strangely enough, with Slim also. The brothers were very down-to-earth and jovial, especially once they'd each had a few beers.

So, while Cody's girlfriend Wendy and Slim's daughter Lisa helped out Charlotte with preparing dinner, the men sat and drank their beers, and watched the NFL game.

Soda in hand and Rocky next to him, Little Jimmy also watched the game.

"I'm not exactly sure those animals are legal as pets in this state," Gary said after a while, pointing at the caged armadillo.

"Most likely not," Slim Mitchell agreed with a laugh. "They ain't even legal in Texas, and they's our state animal."

His younger brother nodded. "The kid just refuses to let the thing go, or I'd have sent it packing back to the wild months ago. So, I indulge him. And when what happened happened . . ."

"So, what did happen?" Gary asked. "Charlotte told me part of it, but what's the full story?"

Cody and Slim told him. Gary laughed until tears were coming out of his eyes. "Oh, my God, oh my dear God!"

"Dude, stop laughing," Slim said. "Getting shot hurts like hell, especially if you accidentally shoot yourself, 'cos then you ain't expecting the bullet to come back at ya."

That just made Gary laugh all the more, so much that the ladies all came out of the kitchen to see what the ruckus was all about.

Everyone had a nice dinner and chatted and laughed, and soon it was time for bed. There were two extra bedrooms in the house. Cody and Wendy got one of those, and Slim got the other. Lisa slept on the living room couch, and Jimmy on the living room floor.

It was a lovely pleasant night. The last such night for most of the people in the house.

CHAPTER 8

"That darn leash don't really look secure," Lisa said, when Jimmy let Rocky out of his cage the next morning to take the armadillo for a short walk outside. Lisa was still wary of Rocky

"I don't believe I've ever seen one of those before," Gary Bentley said. "Where'd you get it?"

"It's homemade," Cody explained. "I borrowed it from a friend so we don't have to keep Rocky in his cage all the while we're in the woods."

Gary nodded and bent down to examine the restraint. It was a simple leather thong that went around either of the armadillo's rear legs above the foot. Padded on the inside to avoid chafing, the collar was securely tightened and buckled in place.

"Looks secure enough to me," Gary judged. "But I'm no expert on this."

"Dad, are those . . . raccoons?" Jimmy asked suddenly, pointing towards the front door.

Cody looked towards the front door himself, saw the group of animals pawing at the entrance, and then gave their host an enquiring stare.

Gary shrugged. "Yep, they're coons all right. Charlotte treats them like pets too." He turned towards the kitchen. "Hey, honey, the raccoons are waiting for their breakfasts."

Soon, Charlotte emerged with Lisa in tow, both carrying packs of cereal and several feeding bowls.

Tugging Rocky along behind him, Jimmy hurried after them both for a look.

Rocky and the raccoons didn't get along. When Charlotte attempted to feed them together, the raccoons pushed the armadillo out of the way and hogged all of the breakfast cereal for themselves. Rocky just stood there watching.

Lisa began laughing.

Jimmy wondered what his grown-up cousin thought was so funny about the raccoons picking on Rocky. Cousin Lisa was so weird at times; for one thing, Jimmy didn't understand why she ran after young men like that, as if it was all adult life consisted of. More than once, Jimmy had seen her kissing one of the young ranch hands named Matt. He decided he'd threaten to tell on her to Uncle Slim if she ever laughed at Rocky again.

"Don't mind 'em, Rocky," he told the nine-banded armadillo. "The coons are just jealous 'cos you're bulletproof, and they ain't."

***

After Charlotte had fed the raccoons, everyone else had breakfast.

Then, Gary, who had an afternoon shift today, prepared to take the visitors over to the Sleepaway Campground.

"It's a lovely place," he told Cody as they left the house together. "First off, there's a great view of the mountains. And then there's the river, which is clear enough at points that you can see its bottom. Great for swimming. Say, do you wanna rent a cabin for your stay here?"

"Nope," Wendy replied. "Cody and I have had more than enough of living cooped indoors."

Cody nodded and gestured to their camper. "Lots of sleeping space in there for anyone who's house-sick. And we also brought one of those house-like tents, 'cos neither Wendy nor Lisa wanna get their hair wet if it rains."

Gary laughed. "Alright then. Let's hit the road." He stared for a moment at Rocky the armadillo while Jimmy carried the creature, which was now back in its cage again, into the camper.

True, the armadillo seemed a harmless enough creature. But Gary was used to seemingly harmless animals becoming nightmares once they came in contact with the drug called Agent Orange. And that nightmare drug had a way of somehow finding its way over to the Sleepaway Campground where his wife's cousin, her boyfriend, and his family were now headed.

CHAPTER 9

"So here we are," Gary Bentley told Cody and his family. "You guys all go ahead and get settled in, and I'll check in on you from time to time."

"Thanks a lot,' Cody said, shaking Gary's hand. "You've been a great help."

Gary smiled and waved it off. "Oh, think nothing of it. After all, you're practically family."

Slim laughed. "Yeah, that is true. But thanks for all your hospitality anyways."

Gary shook Slim's hand, too, and turned to leave. "Remember, now, just call me if you need anything."

"We will," Wendy said. "Thanks again."

Gary nodded and walked off.

Then, just before he stepped back onto the east camping trail that led to the parking lot, he stopped and looked back at the campers. No one was looking his way. Except for Slim, who was seated on a rock, everyone was helping unfurl the camping tent. Gary wasn't looking their way anyway. He was staring at the animal that young Jimmy Mitchell had on that custom-designed leash. The armadillo lay there beside the kid like it was a dog. It seemed to have fallen asleep on the grass.

Gary had no idea why, but once again, the sight of that armadillo was giving him an uneasy feeling.

But leashed up like they've got it, there's no way it's gonna get into Agent Orange, is there? he wondered and finally walked off again.

CHAPTER 10

"Wow, this truly is a lovely place," Lisa told her father after the ranger had left.

Slim Mitchell nodded to his daughter. "Yeah, it sure is, hon."

Gary Bentley had guided the family to a spot near the Campground's east bridge. It had been a long walk, but at this point, the land was regularly flat, like it had been graded. There weren't as many trees as at the camping area nearer to the parking lot. In addition to having a fantastic view of the mountains opposite, without any cabins in the way, there was also a natural stone slope leading down to a relatively shallow area of the Tygart Valley River.

"Feel free to go swimming in there at your leisure," the ranger had told them. "At this part of the river, your feet will hardly even get muddy."

"Sorry, Daddy, but it looks like you won't be sleeping in the camper," Lisa said. "It's too far away for you to walk from here each night and then back again in the morning."

Slim Mitchell grimaced and nodded. Though well on the way back to full health, that darn bullet still occasionally demanded its toll of pain from him. He looked again over at the glorious landscape. Then he stopped looking at it and instead watched his brother and Wendy inflate the tent.

It was a huge family tent with three main partitions (or rooms) and lots of sleeping space.

Jimmy was over there too, trying to be of help but mostly getting in the way, until his daddy told him to go walk his pet 'dillo, but not to go out of sight.

Because it hurt Slim Mitchell to bend over, he couldn't help set up anything. Even carrying lightweight stuff from the camper hurt like he'd just suffered a hernia. After watching him grunt in pain, Cody and Wendy ordered him to sit on a rock while they took care of what needed to be done.

So, Slim had sat on the rock Wendy had pointed out and watched the others work. Lisa had been on her way back to the parking lot now to get a stock of food for lunch when she'd stopped beside her father.

"Okay, Daddy. I'm going to the parking lot now. Do you want anything from the camper?"

Slim first shook his head. But then he remembered something:

"Hey, Lisa, what was it you and that young man was talkin' 'bout back over there at the parking lot?" Slim asked his daughter, with a sideways glance at her.

Lisa pretended nonchalance. "Oh, you mean Toby?"

"If that's his name, yeah."

She shrugged. "I thought I recognized him from somewhere on the internet, but I was wrong. He and his girlfriend are here camping too. Gave me his phone number. We might get together later to drink some beers."

Slim scowled at Lisa. "That's fine, girlie. So long as beers is all you do."

Lisa rolled her eyes. "Dad, I'm grown up now. I'm not in fucking high school any longer."

"Hon, I just don't want you doing any more of those drugs. I'm fine with you smoking all the pot you like, but please . . . please . . ."

Lisa frowned and folded her arms across her breasts. "Daddy, please!"

Slim sighed. "Maybe I am being too watchful over you, girlie, but I can't help it. I don't want you, my only daughter, intentionally messing up your own head."

Lisa nodded dutifully. "Okay, daddy, I understand. You're just concerned about me."

"Exactly."

"Don't worry, I won't let you down. I won't do anything illegal or dangerous."

Slim frowned and studied her face to see if she was lying to him. "Promise?"

"Promise. Oh, come on, Daddy, don't look so serious. We're here to have fun."

Yes, Lisa Mitchell had promised her father she wouldn't do any drugs on this camping trip. But she had every intention of doing some. Her initial plan had been to go looking for campers her age—early twenties—to go have fun with, so she didn't get stuck with her father all day long. But it looked like fortune had already smiled on her. Toby Miller, the young man she'd met at the parking lot, had let her know that he and his girlfriend Alice had 'something good.'

"Coke?" she'd asked excitedly. Because she still lived at home with her father, it had been ages since she'd had any cocaine.

"Much better than coke," Toby had replied. But before she could enquire further, Toby's girlfriend Alice had gotten out of the car, too. Alice looked like she thought Lisa was attempting to seduce Toby, so Lisa had left, but only after getting a good description from Toby of where the pair would be setting up camp.

So that's taken care of, Lisa thought. *First, though, I've gotta get Dad comfortably set up here!*

Full of anticipation of exciting times ahead, Lisa once more hurried over to the Sleepaway Campground's parking lot.

CHAPTER 11

Jimmy Mitchell was discovering one reason why armadillos spent so much time underground: they slept a lot. He'd tried to coax Rocky into walking around like a dog would, but Rocky wasn't having it. The moment Jimmy stopped to examine a rock, or to roll over a fallen branch to peek underneath it, Rocky laid down again and dozed off. Then Jimmy had to rouse him, and they resumed walking.

Dad said not to go out of sight, Jimmy thought, looking back at their tent, which was now completely inflated. His father and Miss Wendy were knocking tent pegs into the ground, and the noise of the mallet whacks seemed to echo off of the nearby mountain range.

The only time that Rocky really came alive on their little walk was when Jimmy unearthed an insect nest under a branch. Then, the armadillo seemed to have drunk coffee. It began digging and eating, consuming the insects faster than Jimmy could count their numbers. It also ate up a few worms unfortunate enough to be in the vicinity. Jimmy watched all of this in delight. He was gonna have tales to tell Tommy Lee when he was back home in Destin, Texas.

Finally, after making sure that his father could still see him, Jimmy sat down on the riverbank. Rocky, his belly now full of food, fell totally asleep beside Jimmy.

Jimmy sat on the riverbank and thought about his dad and Miss Wendy. He hoped they'd get married; then he'd have a mom again just like the other kids at school did. His real mother had died when he was two years old and he didn't even remember her. He just knew from pictures that she'd been really pretty.

But Miss Wendy was really nice too. So, Jimmy hoped that she'd soon be his new mom.

After a while, Jimmy turned his attention to the river. It flowed west at a lazy pace. Uncle Bentley, the park ranger, had said there was a lake at its far end with lots of fishing boats. Jimmy would have liked to walk along the river until he reached the lake, but he knew his dad would be angry if he did. He thought that maybe he'd ask Uncle Slim if he could walk there with him tomorrow.

And then, staring at the water, Jimmy remembered something that Tommy Lee had told him, right after they'd gotten Rocky.

"They say 'dillos can walk underneath water," Tommy Lee had said.

"They can't, they'll die if they do," Jimmy had retorted.

"It's true, they can," Tommy Lee said. "I saw it on TV once. The TV woman said 'dillos can hold their breath for ages."

If that was the case, then it had to be true. TV was where all the real and cool things happened, like cartoons, superheroes, and Spy-Kids.

"Okay, I believe you then," Jimmy had agreed. "Let's try it out."

"Yeah," Tommy Lee agreed. "Let's try it out."

So, they'd hatched a plan to drop the armadillo in a bathtub of water when they were the only ones at home, and then see what happened.

But that was the week when Miss Wendy fell ill and was home all the time, and so they never got the chance. And being little boys, by the time Miss Wendy was well again, the scheme had left their young minds.

But now, staring at the gently flowing waters of the Tygart Valley River, Jimmy wondered what would happen if he dropped Rocky in the river. Would he sink like a stone and then begin walking on the river bed?

This time, what stopped Jimmy from trying the experiment out was the fact that Rocky was fast asleep. Jimmy didn't think Rocky would wake up even if he was dropped in the water. In fact, Rocky was so deeply asleep after that meal of bugs and worms that Jimmy had to pick him up and carry him back over to the tent and then lock the armadillo in his cage.

CHAPTER 12

In their tent this morning, Toby once again counted the packages of Agent Orange he and Alice had stolen from Eddie Bush.

"There's eight of them," he told Alice. "But last night I could've sworn there was more 'orange' in each of them."

Alice nodded. "Yeah, me too. But remember we got really high last night. So maybe we used more than we thought we did. Must have been the heat of our desperation, you know?"

Toby gave her a suspicious look. "Yeah, maybe you're right, babe. Maybe you're right." Then he frowned at the stash again. "We'd better be careful how we use it then. This stuff ain't gonna last us forever."

Alice frowned. "I know, I know. Stop looking at me like that. You've smoked up more of it than I have."

Toby shook his head. "No, that's not what I'm thinking, babe."

She gave him a narrow look. "What then?"

"I'm just thinking that this is a really little thing to lose one's life over, like Carlos did."

Alice thought about that for a moment, then shrugged. "Maybe, but we did what we had to do. Can't make an omelet with unbroken eggs like they say."

Toby nodded. "Yeah, that's right."

"Hey, speaking of eggs," Alice said. "I'm gonna make us some for breakfast. While I fry up the eggs and bacon, you better call Johnny at the bar."

Toby looked confused. "What the hell for?"

"Ask after Carlos. Tell him we're looking for him to buy some weed, and he's not picking up his phone. That way, we'll know if there's any news."

Toby nodded and picked his phone up from the ground beside his sleeping bag. While Alice watched him, Toby phoned Johnny at the Whistle Stop Bar, and they both spoke for a few minutes.

"What's he say?" she asked afterward.

Toby shrugged. "Nothing. He's not heard from Carlos either since last night. They were supposed to hang out with Leslie and Rosa after Johnny got off from work, but Carlos no-showed. Johnny called Eddie Bush's bodyguard Mo this morning, but Mo told him the boss sent Carlos to Utah late last night to handle some emergency business for him, and he won't be back for several months."

Alice nodded. "Looks like the cover-up has already gone into effect."

Toby nodded back at her. "Yeah, we're in the clear, babe." He gestured out at the camping stove they'd brought along. "What's happening to our breakfast?"

"I forgot. I'll get started on it right away. No, not right away. I need to do something else first."

Toby shrugged. "Don't take too long at whatever it is. I'm starving; it feels like I haven't eaten for days."

"Man, we're junkies. Neither of us have eaten for days."

Shaking his head at her, Toby crawled out of the tent entrance.

Looking at her boyfriend had alerted Alice to a possible alteration in her own face. While Toby stretched and stared across the river at the nearby mountains, Alice Brown hurriedly got a powder compact out of her purse and examined herself critically in it.

The long blonde hair, the cold blue eyes, the cynical lips, the overall skinny and wasted appearance. All of those she was very familiar with. But not so much with this new difference.

Now, like flowers blooming orange in a garden of pink skin, her eyes had really brightened up; like she'd just noticed in Toby. Alice winced; the orange eyes were the main thing she hated about using 'orange.' They were such a fashion crisis.

She decided that the first chance they got to return to town, they were both buying sunglasses. Anyone looking at them now would instantly know something was off about them.

***

With nothing to do for the next few days except pray no one had noticed them entering and leaving Eddie Bush's house last night, it wasn't long before both Toby and Alice grew bored. Normally this shouldn't have been a problem—they had sufficient Agent Orange to last them a week, two weeks if they didn't burn through it all, like they were doing now.

Since after breakfast, both of them had been cracking it up. They lay there in the sunshine with their crack pipes, with a bag of orange between them on the beach towel and just let it rip.

This was junkie paradise, just how it was meant to be. From here, you might die and go to hell, but you'd definitely enjoy the ride.

The bliss of the drug was undeniable, but once the short burst of euphoria ended, the accompanying neurosis and paranoia set in. In the vicious cycle of Agent Orange addiction, the sole cure for the paranoia was more of the drug, which in turn increased the intensity of the delusional state of mind.

Toby and Alice had had spats in the past; all junkies did. But back then, neither of them had had access to the amount of drugs that they did now. So, the more orange crack they did, the worse their mental deterioration became, until soon Toby, with suspecting eyes, was watching from behind every tree, and Alice thought the people in the online soap she was watching on her cellphone were watching her in return.

And because Alice was watching a soap opera about adultery, it wasn't long before her mind made a link between the sleazy onscreen wives and the young woman they'd met at the parking lot earlier today.

"Hey, Toby, you can't pull the wool over my eyes any longer," Alice said suddenly, sitting up on the large beach towel they were both sharing and staring daggers at her boyfriend.

Toby, who'd been trying to determine if the eyes he knew were staring at him from the trees belonged to a bigfoot or a giant raccoon, turned to stare at her in confusion.

"What the hell you talkin' 'bout, babe?" he asked. "What wool?"

"I know you're planning on cheating on me," Alice told him. "You're gonna cheat on me with that big-tit slut we met this morning, aren't you?"

"Shit, Alice, don't you dare start up with that jealous nonsense again!"

Alice made a stabbing motion with her crack pipe. "I swear to God, Toby, if you dare hit on that girl Lisa, I'll cut your damn balls off. God help me, I will!"

Alice looked mad enough to stab him with the glass pipe. And the noise she was making—not the accusation, which was accurate enough, but the noise—was filling up Toby's brain like a chainsaw cutting wood. Toby felt like killing Alice, and he might have done so there and then had he not noticed that the bag of Agent Orange they'd both been sharing was now empty.

"Fuck you, Alice!" he told her, leaping to his feet.

"Yeah, like you even bother to anymore," she spat back, the skin of her face tight and her expression ugly.

She looked really ugly like this and Toby wondered what he'd ever seen in her in the first place. She was nothing like that cute girl Lisa they'd met this morning. Of course, in Toby's state of heightened delusion, he'd overlooked the fact that in the normal state of affairs and a non-chemically adjusted frame of mind, Alice was much prettier than Lisa was.

Anyway, Toby rushed away from the Alice chainsaw noise in his head into the tent, glad also to escape the watching eyes and also the damning knowledge that soon, very soon indeed, the police were going to arrive here in the company of Carlos's parents and entire family and Rosa and Johnny and Eddie Bush also and were going to beat the crap out of Alice and himself for killing their beloved citizen, son, friend, boyfriend, employee, drug-runner and whatever.

"I'm fucking warning you, Toby," Alice ranted on. "If I see you the fuck anywhere near that bitch, I'll—"

Her voice now seemed jet-engine loud, but Toby managed to tune her out. This wasn't exactly difficult to accomplish, as he'd just made the discovery that part of their Agent Orange stash was missing.

There had been eight bags in all and now there were only five. Mixed in with his fear of the FBI and Al Qaeda and whoever else would be looking for Carlos's slayers to have their revenge, Toby wasn't certain any more.

"But I know there were more than five in here for sure," he said aloud.

He looked around for the missing packages. Maybe they'd spilled somewhere. But he couldn't see them anywhere.

"Hey, Alice, did you hide the orange somewhere?"

"What? Hide what, you cheating asshole? And don't you dare change the subject! I mean it, if I—"

"Alice, shut up, dammit! The orange is missing!"

CHAPTER 13

On hearing that, Alice shut up and came running. She still looked incensed with Toby, but she looked worried, too.

"What do you mean our orange is missing?" she demanded once she was by his side.

Toby pointed down at the plastic bag in which the stash was stored. "Count them yourself."

Alice crouched down beside the bag and counted. "One . . . two . . . three . . . four . . . five." She looked up at Toby. "The hell's the matter with you, man? It's all here."

"No, it isn't all here, you crackhead! Some of it is missing!"

"In your dreams." Alice straightened up again. "Babe, you always were crap at arithmetic. That's all the orange that we had. I thought you called me in here for something serious."

But Toby, who was now wading knee-deep in a swamp of chemically-induced paranoia, wasn't about to let the matter go. He was certain there had been more Agent Orange in the bag to begin with, although he couldn't remember how much it had been.

"No, no, no, no, no," he told Alice firmly. "Someone took the rest of the orange. It was either you or me, or someone else came in here and stole it."

"Just listen to yourself," Alice replied. "You sound crazy. Nobody came in here and took anything away. It's been just you and me here all day." Then, her previous irritation with him returned to her mind. "Stop changing the subject—if you're planning on sharing our Agent Orange with that slut, well, you can forget about it, 'cos I'm not gonna stand for it. This is *our* orange. *We* worked for it. *We* alone fucking get to use it."

"*You* fucking stop changing the subject!" Toby thundered at her, which made Alice glare at him in equal anger.

"Okay, okay, baby," she angrily agreed. "But, hey, man, don't you dare blame me for the theft. Maybe it was a raccoon that took it. Remember that story Johnny told us, about the raccoon that got into some orange out here and fucked up a bunch of campers? How about if the ranger guy killed the wrong raccoon!?" By now, Alice was almost yelling at Toby. "What if the real crackhead raccoon is still out here in these woods, stealing people's orange and killing 'em!?" Hands on hips, she stared him down. "How 'bout considering that explanation, huh, Sherlock!?"

"I don't goddamn think you stole the Agent Orange," Toby replied Alice. "But *I do* need you to stop fucking yelling at me, you bitch!"

"Fuck you, Toby!"

"Goddamn shut the hell up, Alice! Your horrible voice is driving me crazy!"

While making this declaration, Toby had a murderous gleam in his orange eyes. Alice had noticed it, too. Even though the rage in her was equal to his and right now she wanted to murder Toby too, a small corner of her mind accepted the fact that he was too big for her to kill without her switchblade knife, and as the knife was in her handbag, which was currently somewhere out of sight, the wise thing for her to do was to flee from Toby now and return to kill him later.

So, Alice turned to run. But Toby was too fast for her. Before she could crawl her way out of their tent, he was on top of her. She felt his hands wrap themselves around her throat, and then he'd cut off her air supply, and she was dying, plain and simple.

She was enraged to be dying, wishing she did have her knife and could dig his eyes out with it, and afterward cut his balls off, and then gut him, and then . . .

But then the lights all faded out for her.

CHAPTER 14

Rocky the armadillo was rather confused by his new environment. It was exciting, its smells conflicting with those he associated with the place he regarded as home. Here the soil was wet, moist rather than dry, and he wanted to dig, dig, dig, to tear up that soft earth with his claws and make himself an extensive burrow, where he could eat all the worms and insects he desired.

But this 'littler home' he was stuck in now, with its wire walls, was frustrating all his attempts to get free. The restraint on his ankle was also a problem, but not as pressing a problem as the need to be outside of his cage for good.

Like all armadillos, Rocky had weak eyesight. But he recognized the people near him by their smells—the adults and the child. The child was his friend, and he was certain that if the adults weren't nearby, the child would free him of both his cage and the leg restraint and permit him to roam about and do as he pleased.

Rocky bent and chewed at the leg restraint. To his surprise, it was soft. He tugged on it and felt like it was slipping free of his leg. But then the boy returned with food and water for him, and for a while, he ate and drank and put aside his instinctive desire for freedom.

CHAPTER 15

"Yeah, you got exactly what you deserved, you stupid noisy bitch!" Toby snarled down at Alice's lifeless body. "I should've done this a long time ago. Rid myself of you for good."

Toby remained like that, crouched down beside his dead girlfriend, for a few minutes. Then he left Alice's side and returned to the bag of Agent Orange. He popped two chunks of the drug into his mouth, sat down, and chewed them.

He still felt paranoid, but now there wasn't any grating Alice noise to contend with either. But of course, the eyes amidst the trees outside would be waiting and watching him, waiting and watching.

I'd better pull Alice out of sight, so no one sees her.

So, Toby dragged Alice back into their tent and draped their camping mattress over her. He next arranged their bags and pillows to make things look natural in there. Then he walked back over to the package of orange crack. What to do about it?

Toby agreed with Alice's theory that maybe a raccoon had broken in here and had stolen some of the drugs because, despite what she had said, there really had been more at the start. But that was water under the bridge now.

What is important now is that I prevent any more of such stealing. With Alice dead now, all this remaining orange is mine and mine alone! But where the hell do I store it so the raccoons don't get at it again? Under the mattress? Inside our bags? No, I've got the perfect answer. Back at the car will be best.

Toby decided to head for the parking lot right there and then. Keeping back one package of Agent Orange for today's use, he rolled up the rest of the drug into a tight package and stuck it in his jacket pocket. Then, after making sure that any casual observer wouldn't notice Alice's body hidden beneath the bedding, he exited the tent and zipped up the entrance after him.

Just a quick trip there and back, he told himself.

***

Toby walked quickly, determined that those he felt were watching wouldn't have their way with him.

He and Alice had camped almost as far from the campground parking lot as the Mitchell family, but on the other side of the east trail. Because Toby was wary of drawing attention to himself, he walked not on the trail itself but alongside it.

No one else seemed to be camping on this side of the trail at the moment, but a junkie who'd just murdered his girlfriend, had a dangerous narcotic in his pocket, and also had delusions that the US government was watching him, couldn't be too careful.

So, Toby made his careful way along the trail. But halfway there, he felt the call of nature. In fact, all of a sudden it felt like he was about to poop his pants. With his paranoia adding to the sense of urgency in his gut, Toby practically ran through the woods to a nearby tree that wasn't visible from the camping trail. Then he just got down his pants in time.

After he was done wiping his ass clean, Toby got up again and resumed his solitary trek to the car park. Taking a dump seemed to have reduced his anxiety. But just when he realized that the U.S. government wouldn't actually be watching him amidst these trees, another worry hit him:

I hope that hot chick Lisa doesn't come looking for me while I'm away. How the hell am I gonna explain Alice's corpse to her?

He was already at the car park now, and so could hurry right back to his campsite.

After a quick look left and right, Toby walked onto the parking lot, hurried quickly past Lisa's family's parked RV, and reached his own car. After getting his key from his pocket and unlocking the car door, Toby suddenly realized that he didn't have the bag of Agent Orange with him.

He stood there for a long while, trying to work out where he'd lost it. Had he forgotten to take it out of the tent at all?

No, it was in my pocket then. I remember feeling it in there. Shit! So, where the hell did I drop it?

Half-crazed with worry about that much precious drug going to waste, Toby ran all the way back to where he'd taken a dump. When he didn't find the drug there, he searched the area in a widening circle. Then he went back to the tent and searched there, too, but the missing Agent Orange wasn't there either; only the portion he'd reserved for today's usage was. He ate a few chunks of those and then, feeling reenergized, hurried back to search some more.

Toby searched back and forth in the woods until night fell, and then he decided to quit. Standing there in the darkness, with the wind rustling the leaves around him, he considered his miserable plight, how all of the hard work and killing had been for nothing.

I've been searching for five hours now, and haven't found the damn drugs. Shit! How could I have been so damn careless?

Despondent at losing the Agent Orange, he walked back to the tent. To put himself in a better mood once there, he got out a chunk of orange from the meager surviving pack of the drug and loaded it into his crack pipe.

After inhaling the fumes for a while, things didn't seem so bad anymore. Still, cracking up was making him angry as hell at whoever had found and 'stolen' his lost orange. If he encountered that person, there'd be hell to pay. Heads would roll and blood would flow for certain.

After smoking up another chunk of Agent Orange, Toby walked into the tent and dragged Alice's body out of it.

Now that the moon was out, and everyone around would be getting ready to go to sleep, it was time to go bury the noisy bitch.

CHAPTER 16

The Mitchell family's evening was calm and uneventful. All of the adults drank beer, sang campfire songs, and told stories.

"I wish I was old enough to drink beer, too," Jimmy whispered to Rocky as he watched his elders laugh around the campfire. "It seems to make people very happy."

Jimmy had Rocky outside his cage on his leash again. Seeing as he was sitting on a tree stump around the campfire like the others, he'd secured the armadillo's leash to one of the cage doors so it could walk around because it didn't seem to enjoy the campfire as much as humans did.

Uncle Bentley, or 'Uncle Ranger' as Jimmy now liked to think of him, had earlier stopped by their campsite on his way home. Jimmy decided he'd like to be a park ranger too when he grew up.

"Then, no one can keep me from having the pets that I want," he told Rocky. "You and I and all of the other armadillos in Texas can go camping whenever we want."

"So," Wendy was saying, "last night Charlotte told Lisa and me this creepy story about a killer raccoon. Apparently, it got addicted to some narcotic and killed a whole bunch of campers in these same woods."

Slim Mitchell laughed. "A killer raccoon? C'mon, Wendy, you gotta know she was just pulling your leg."

But Lisa shook her head emphatically. "Daddy, it's true. Charlotte said Uncle Gary was the one that finally killed the killer raccoon."

"Wow," Slim said, looking over at Jimmy and his roving pet. "Terrorist 'dillos and now serial-killin' coons. What's the world gonna think of next?"

"Easy Slim," Cody Mitchell cautioned. "Don't ya go gettin' all worked up now. Remember, what happened back at home was just a misunderstanding, that's all."

Slim scowled. "Yeah, yeah, alright." Then he looked at Lisa. "Get me another beer, girl."

***

It was at around midnight that Rocky the armadillo escaped from his cage.

Escape was easy enough. The armadillo simply got restless, and while pushing against the cage bars in an exploratory attempt to understand why they were so resistant to its claws, it accidentally sprung the latch. The reason this was possible was because Jimmy, who'd been very tired by the time he was rehousing Rocky, hadn't taken the time to untie the end of Rocky's leash that he'd secured to the cage door. The rope being in the way meant that the latch hadn't closed and locked properly. And so, the armadillo's nosing about had popped it open again.

Leaving the cage this time also resulted in Rocky's snagging the buckle of his foot-collar on a metal protrusion, which, when the armadillo tugged the foot forward, burst the buckle. Thus, by a series of unfortunate events, the armadillo was suddenly free in the room of the tent that he shared with Jimmy.

Jimmy was, of course, fast asleep and was oblivious to the sound of his pet getting free.

The freed armadillo instinctively walked over to Jimmy's side and peered down at him for a while, and the lure of familiarity almost made Rocky lie down beside Jimmy and fall asleep himself.

But then, the smells of the forest and sounds of the night creatures called to the armadillo's senses. And once its animal instincts were thus roused, its semi-domesticized behavior was lost, for a while at least.

Rocky nosed around Jimmy's room for a while, seeking a way outside, and finally clawed his way out to freedom through the tent fabric.

***

Out in the wild, Rocky first reacquainted himself with freedom. The world now seemed so vast, so immense, so different from the constrained world of human-created enclosures, although the enclosures provided regular food and safety from predators.

Rocky walked down to the riverside and drank long and deep from the flowing water, sniffing at the night insects that skimmed over the water's surface but were too far off for him to catch and eat.

Then, the armadillo turned and climbed back up the river bank and wandered off into the forest. Soon Rocky had left Jimmy and the Mitchells well behind him and was exploring this forest like crazy, rooting under dropped branches and tree roots for grubs and worms, and once even finding a rotting apple crawling with worms, which provided him with both plant and animal nutrition.

Soon, the little armadillo's belly was full and he was wondering what to do with himself. As far as he could tell, there were no other armadillos around here, just a lot of those funny doglike creatures with black bands across their eyes that had interfered with his feeding that morning.

It was at that point that he smelled a strange odor that seemingly compelled him to investigate it.

And that was how Rocky the armadillo located Toby's missing stash of Agent Orange, which had fallen out of his jacket pocket while he'd been relieving himself in the woods and then rolled out of sight beneath some bushes and into a small hole.

Rocky didn't know what he'd found, only that it smelled good to eat. So, the armadillo tucked in.

CHAPTER 17

There was no consistency to what Agent Orange did in the bodies of the animal species that consumed it. Other than for their eyes turning bright orange and their suddenly developing a crazed tendency to violence, that was.

In Rocky the armadillo's case, at first nothing appeared to happen. Seemingly unable to stop himself, Rocky ate and ate the waxy orange chunks, ripping open another pack before he'd even finished the previous one. There was simply too much of the drug available to him, however, and with his belly already full of worms and grubs before he'd found this strange new food, he finally stopped eating.

Then, he stood there for a while, wondering in his animal way why he felt so odd. This was followed by a sense of alarm that maybe he was in danger here, amongst the other woodland creatures, followed by the desire to return to the company of his human protectors, where he'd be safe.

Rocky took four steps in the direction of the Mitchell family's campsite and then toppled over. The armadillo had fallen asleep on his feet. Coincidentally, he rolled back into the same hole where the Agent Orange had itself fallen.

Down in the hole, while the unwary campers slept nearby, Agent Orange worked its strange and nasty work on the unconscious armadillo.

First of all, the substance made the armadillo bigger. Not much larger, because of restrictions caused by its horny shell, but a large enough difference in size to be easily noticeable.

Then, it made Rocky stronger. Much stronger.

But the drug's most problematic effect was that it removed the armadillo's natural timidity, and instead replaced it with the classic

48

orangehead's borderline psychotic mental state; a state in which violence seemed as natural a process as eating, drinking, and getting high. A deranged mental state in which right and wrong became indistinguishable, and killing, or at least inflicting grievous bodily damage on others, was as normal as breathing air.

By the time Rocky the armadillo woke up again, he'd become an extremely dangerous animal.

Sure, little Jimmy Mitchell's pet armadillo had been considered a 'wild' animal before, but now he truly was WILD.

CHAPTER 18

"Dad, Rocky's missing!" was the cry that startled Cody and Wendy the next morning.

"Missing? How?" Cody asked, after picking himself up from eating Wendy's pussy.

Jimmy was calling from inside of the middle tent room where he'd slept. His little body was pressed up against the fabric partition that separated the rooms, but Cody knew the boy would soon leave his own sleeping space and come round to his and Wendy's.

He wiped his mouth, mumbled, "Sorry, hon, later," at Wendy, and then rolled over to his side of the mattress.

As Cody had expected, a few seconds later, Jimmy unzipped their own entrance, burst into their 'room', and stood there, gesturing wildly about.

"Rocky's gone, Dad!"

"All right, calm down, boy, and tell me exactly what happened," his father said.

Jimmy didn't calm down. "He slipped his leash and ran off! Dad, we gotta find him!"

Cody listened and then nodded. "All right, son, now this is what you'll do. Go and wait for me and Miss Wendy outside the tent, and don't you dare come back inside till we're done working out how to find Rocky again."

Wendy leaned up on her elbow and whispered something in Cody's ear.

"Yeah, that's right, son. Go wake up your Uncle Slim and tell him exactly what happened and that we'll need to go find Rocky once we've all had our breakfasts."

"And remember, Jimmy," Wendy added, "you don't come back inside here, except your father or myself call for you. You got that?"

"Okay, Miss Wendy," Jimmy said and ran off again.

"Think that gives us enough time to finish what we'd started?" Cody asked Wendy, getting up to seal the tent entrance again.

"I sure hope so," she replied in a throaty and lusty voice. "I know 'dillos like holes, but it sure ain't in the one between my legs where you were searching earlier."

Cody laughed. "I'll get right back to checking, ma'am, just to make sure. One can never be certain with little critters like that."

Cody resumed eating Wendy's pussy.

***

By the time Jimmy had reemerged from his father's room, Slim Mitchell was already awake and was pissing against a nearby tree.

Jimmy waited for his uncle to finish urinating and then explained about the missing armadillo.

"Already?" Slim asked once Jimmy had finished. "I knew that 'dillo was up to no good, accompanying us on this trip the way he did. Now look at this. We're just one day into the thing and already he's run off. Stirring things up already. Someone should shoot the damn thing!"

Jimmy gaped at his uncle in fright.

Seeing the horrified expression on his nephew's face, Slim smiled. "Don't worry, boy, we'll find your 'dillo for you. Hey, what's your father up to?"

Jimmy shrugged. "I dunno, Uncle Slim. He and Miss Wendy said they had something to discuss in private before we went out looking for Rocky."

On hearing that, a sly grin came over Slim's features. "Yeah, I know exactly what they'll be discussing, boy."

"What, Uncle Slim?"

"It's about which of three body cavities the 'dillo might be hiding in at the moment. Your dad won't find Rocky in any of 'em, but Wendy sure is gonna enjoy the searching."

"What you talkin' 'bout, Uncle Slim?"

Slim Mitchell laughed. "Don't worry 'bout it, son. You'll understand everything clearly in four or five years' time."

Slim yawned and gestured over at the leftmost tent room, which he was sharing with his daughter. "In the meantime, go wake up Lisa. Tell her the news about Rocky's runnin' off too."

***

"Damn, I don't feel too good," Lisa said, while Jimmy reeled off his tale of woe.

"What's the matter with you, Cousin Lisa?"

"Too much beer, kid."

"But last night, you said the beer was great. You were laughing and joking and carrying on with Dad and Miss Wendy."

Lisa, red-eyed and hungover, sat up on her bedding and frowned at him. "Kid, get the hell outta my sight. Don't worry, we'll find that pesky 'dillo of yours."

CHAPTER 19

"Okay, everyone, let's split up," Cody said after breakfast, when the family had all gathered outside their tent. "Now, we all know that Rocky's missing, and we also all know that this Sleepaway Campground is a huge place. There's no way we'll ever find the armadillo if we're all looking for it together."

From force of habit, Cody and Wendy both had on their ten-gallon hats, though the morning weather was still cool, and the hats made them look 'out of state.'

"How are we going to group ourselves?" Slim asked.

Nodding, Lisa peered up from looking at her cell phone. One of the best things about this particular campground was that she had cell phone reception. Her father and Cody didn't, though, and Wendy's cellphone signal appeared to be patchy at best.

Also, now that Lisa had had breakfast, her hangover was subsiding.

"I'm thinking that Wendy and I should remain together," Cody said. "We'll head east towards the trailer park Gary said exists that way."

"That sounds good to me," Wendy agreed.

"How about me, Daddy?" Jimmy asked. "Who'm I goin' with to search?"

"You'll go with me," Slim said. "We'll walk westward opposite to your daddy, towards the parking lot."

"That leaves me out then," Lisa said. She pointed over to the river. "I doubt armadillos like water much. So, after I get the dishes done, I'll head inland"—she gestured over everyone's heads at the woods —"and see if I can spot Rocky anywhere."

"That sounds like a good plan," Cody agreed. "So, alright, now we know where each grouping is supposed to be searching for Rocky." Then his expression turned a little perplexed. "But what exactly are we supposed to be lookin' for anyway? This place goes on forever. How we gon' know that the 'dillo was nearby?"

Slim scratched his scraggly chin for a bit. "I guess we look for holes in the ground, like in the enclosure at home. The earth around here is soft; won't take Rocky long to hide himself away somewhere. So, we'll look for freshly dug holes."

The others all nodded.

"He'll come if you offer him bacon, too," Jimmy said. "Rocky loves bacon."

"Sorry, Jimmy, but we ate the last bacon in camp for breakfast," Wendy said. "But we'll get some for you later in the day."

Jimmy nodded.

"How long are we all searching for?" Lisa asked.

"Say till about noon," Cody replied to her. "Then we'll all meet up back here again for our lunch."

"Noon it is. Maybe we'll even be in luck and find that Rocky's preceded us back here," Slim agreed.

"Alright, now I know the phone signal around here ain't the most reliable," Cody added on a final note. "But please, try calling the other groups if ya notice anything odd that could have to do with li'l Rocky."

Wendy, Cody, Jimmy and Slim set off east and west as agreed on. Lisa walked over to wash the breakfast pans in the river.

***

Once Lisa got through with cleaning up the breakfast things, she did some quick thinking.

First off, I don't wanna waste my whole morning looking for some dumb 'dillo. Why we had to bring it along in the first place is still a mystery to me. Yeah, so it's Jimmy's li'l pet and he's gonna feel lost without it, but so fucking what?

What Lisa really wanted to do on this vacation was party. She was young, pretty, and hot and didn't intend to spend time looking for holes in the forest floor.

I know where there's a party happening. And since Uncle Cody said we'll meet back here at noon and we're all heading in different directions, there ain't no chance of anyone discovering I didn't go looking for Rocky if I come back here on time.

So, Lisa changed her clothes to a top and set of pants that nicely showed off her figure, put on some makeup, and then, after zipping up the tent entrance, walked off in the same direction she'd earlier indicated she would.

But then, she'd only pointed that way because that direction was where Toby and Alice had said they'd be pitching their own tent.

CHAPTER 20

After pulling into the Sleepaway Campground parking lot that morning, Gary Bentley spent a few minutes working out the morning's itinerary.

First of all, I need to check out those cabins over on the far side of the river. Then there are those two crazy campers, the girl and the boy I saw yesterday afternoon— those two looked like born fire-starters. Might even be druggies, too. Then I'll check on the Mitchells and see how they're doing. I better get all of this in a logical order. All right, I'll start off here at the west side of the park and then head east. That way, I'll arrive at the Mitchell's place at the end of my patrol and be able to sit and chat for a while.

With this decided, Gary set off walking west, down along the riverbank. While walking, he watched the mountain slopes. During the past week, several campers had reported bear sightings. Black bears didn't normally come into the campground, but occasionally, a particularly hungry one might raid the dumpsters near the cabins.

Gary saw no sign of bears on this west side and, after making the connection, headed back along the west park trail. That was out of the way then; time to see what the campers were up to today. Folks could and did do as they pleased in the woods. So long as they weren't littering or starting fires, Gary mostly kept out of everyone's business. He liked the feeling that the people who visited the countryside came to refresh themselves.

Though sometimes, they seem to need recreational drugs to help them achieve peace.

Suddenly, he frowned. Not because he overly disapproved of recreational drugs but because, out of the corner of his eyes, he'd just spotted something unusual.

Or had he?

The creature that Gary may or may not have noticed had been heading eastward, though not exactly parallel to the camping trail Gary was about to set out along. If it existed at all, it had been moving in the direction of the highway that led to the Sleepaway Campground, or maybe towards the Teter Creek Lake trailer park.

That thing looked like a large tortoise. But tortoises can't move that fast. And it had a rather funny shape, too. Sort of like a pig or something . . .

Gary decided his eyes were deceiving him.

CHAPTER 21

The other person who noticed the same strange creature as Gary Bentley was Carolyn Dunnam, who was hiking over from the trailer park to meet up with some friends who were camping beside the river.

Carolyn had been walking for about half an hour when she decided to stop and drink some water. She lowered her backpack and got out a bottle of water from it. Then she sat down to rest her legs and drink her water.

She was looking forward to seeing William, the boy who'd invited her to the camp. She'd been friends with William's sister, Katie, for a while now but had only just met Katie's older brother. And they'd immediately hit it off. At the moment, William was single, and so was she . . .

And he seems as into me as I'm into him, so with any luck, by this time tomorrow, we'll be an item. Huh, what the hell is that?

She frowned at what she'd thought she'd seen walking softly amidst the trees directly ahead of her. It looked like a cross between a tortoise and a pig and . . .

Nah, I'm seeing things, she told herself firmly. *Walking solitary like this in the forest will do that to ya.*

But because Carolyn still heard the rustling of leaves and snapping of underfoot branches, she decided to investigate.

Not wanting to startle the mystery animal, she got to her feet and padded quietly after the unknown creature. After doing her very best to keep quiet, she parted a final set of leaves, and there it was before her. It was standing beside a tree, looking around. And now, she immediately recognized it for what it was.

That's a frigging armadillo! But what's it doing up here in the north? They aren't native to this state, or even this part of the country!

First, she was very surprised, then she was very amused. Then she became slightly worried.

That armadillo looks odd, Carolyn thought as she peered out through the leafy covering and sipped her water. *It seems mutated as if it fell out of a sci-fi comic.*

Though clearly an armadillo, this version was all out of proportion. Firstly, it was much larger than those she was used to seeing on YouTube. Most of those armadillos were the size of little dogs and looked cute and cuddly. This one, however, was about twice as large as that. Carolyn still wouldn't exactly rank it as 'large-dog-sized,' because its legs were quite short, but it had that 'bulldog' sort of ambience; the visuals of a stocky beast with a heavy body.

It would never pass as 'cute,' and did not look 'cuddly' either.

The next thing that struck her as odd, was the way its armor-plating was laid out. She knew that armadillos were classified by the number of bands they had, but in this case, the armor looked all broken up and fused together again, like it was one of those Mutant Ninja Turtles, but without the colored masks. Its claws were massive compared to the size of its feet, which were themselves larger than one would expect for a creature of its size. And finally . . .

What the hell is the deal with its eyes? Why would an armadillo have eyes like that?

The armadillo's eyes reminded Carolyn of a guy she and Katie had seen one night in a bar. That guy's eyes had a weird orange tint to them.

"Orangehead," Katie had explained.

"What?" she'd asked.

"You know, like they've been showing on the news. Orangeheads. Agent Orange addicts. Toby over there is one of 'em."

Carolyn had nodded and continued watching the guy over her drink. She was mostly innocent, where drugs were concerned and hadn't even done pot in high school. Now that she was nearing her college graduation, Katie was forever daring her to try marijuana, but so far Carolyn hadn't had the nerve to do so.

The guy Katie had called Toby had walked over to say hello to Katie and herself. He'd brought his girlfriend with him, a girl named Alice. Alice's eyes had the same orange color as his own.

To Carolyn's mind, that night, the pair of them had seemed pleasant enough, though they definitely also gave off the vibe of being highly strung.

And this creature I'm staring at now definitely seems highly strung to me. And its own eyes are like Toby's and Alice's turned up to maximum brightness.

The armadillo's eyes were huge. They bulged out massively, looking exactly like little orange light bulbs screwed into its head.

All the while that Carolyn had been staring at the armadillo, it had remained motionless. But its legs and neck kept twitching like it was in a state of tension, as if it was trying to make up its mind on what to do next.

After a while of staring at the strange animal, Carolyn decided to take its picture and share it with the people she was journeying to see at the camp. Moving as silently as she could, she pulled her cell phone out of her pocket and unlocked its screen.

Dammit, still no network service around here! One would expect there to be at least one or two bars, considering that the trailer park is nearby.

No network coverage meant that she wouldn't be able to share her pictures with her friends before she arrived at their campsite, but that didn't matter, so long as she got the photos.

Carolyn lifted the cell phone to snap the weird animal and gaped.

The weird-looking armadillo had vanished.

Hey, where'd it suddenly go? And how did it leave there without me hearing it moving off?

The answer to her second question was clearly her complete focus on her cell phone.

But I really want to snap that thing. Otherwise, no one will ever believe me that I actually saw it. It'll be like one of those urban legend things. Armadillos in the West Virginian woods? Yeah, right, soon you'll be telling us tales of Nevada Desert sharks.

The only thing to do would be to find the damn armadillo. So, Carolyn hurried back to where she'd dropped her backpack, shrugged herself back into it, and then retraced her steps toward where the weird creature had been standing.

Though Carolyn had no experience in animal tracking, she soon found a set of large animal footprints that easily matched the beast she was after. The footprints, however, diverted away from her route to the Sleepaway Campground. She shrugged at this.

It isn't like I can ever get lost out here; I know this area of the countryside like the back of my hand.

So, she set off after the armadillo, still doing her best to keep quiet so as not to scare it away.

Then, after about two minutes, she reached her destination. The armadillo tracks led to a hole in the ground. A very large hole that was maybe a foot and a half in width.

Now, this was unexpected, she thought and drank some more water.

Carolyn felt rather frustrated on seeing that the armadillo had entered its hole. It would really be great if she could get a picture of it. And so, after checking out the time on her wristwatch, she decided to sit and wait nearby, just in case the armadillo came out of its hole again.

I'll give myself an hour's wait, and after that I'll set off again for the camp. But I'll first of all mark two of these nearby trees so that I can locate this hole again.

And so, Carolyn Dunnam sat down and waited. So as not to get bored, Carolyn passed the time reading. Here, finally, the internet seemed to be working, and so, after sending a message over to Katie telling her she'd gotten sidetracked on her way over but promising her a 'surprise that would be worth it,' she googled 'armadillos' and began reading. Occasionally, Carolyn would stare over at the large hole in the ground and wish the armadillo would hurry up and show itself.

She found her reading very interesting. But then she reached the point where it was written that 'armadillos often have more than one hole to their burrows.'

On reading this, Carolyn realized she was wasting her time by sitting here like this. She put away her cell phone and got to her feet.

The damn creature may have left by another exit. Tomorrow, maybe, if I can convince Katie and William that I'm not pranking them, I'll bring them over here, and we can all search for the armadillo's other holes. But how do I mark this place so we'll easily locate it?

Then Carolyn turned around and saw the creature she'd been stalking standing just five yards away from her and staring at her.

Her first reaction was surprise, and then she felt overjoyed. Oh no, she wouldn't be leaving without her pictures after all.

In fact, with the way it's standing there like that, unafraid of me, I may even be able to make a video of it.

But then Carolyn got the clear vibe that the armadillo was angry with her. This of course made no sense to her, but it did bring back to her mind something Katie had told her that night when they'd met Toby in the bar.

Katie said orangeheads are irrationally violent, and can be stirred up to murderous impulses by the slightest provocation; even if it's unintentional. I won't go out on a limb here, but from the look of this animal's eyes, it does seem possible that it's gotten addicted to the same drug Toby was on.

The way the armadillo was looking at her, struck her now as very wrong. She realized also that it wasn't exactly standing upright, but that its legs were bent, the rear pair more than the front set . . .

. . . *As if it plans on charging at me,* she realized in sudden fright.

She turned and ran. A few seconds later, she heard the sound of the armadillo charging after her. In a panic, Carolyn turned to look at the armadillo. It was gaining on her.

Shit!

She looked forward again, but not in time to change her direction.

Carolyn ran right into a tree that stood in her way and knocked herself out.

She stood there, upright but unconscious, for a second, and then gravity pulled her down to the ground.

In a flash, the armadillo was on her and was digging its claws into her body, ripping her skin open, shredding flesh from bone, and bloodily pulling her internal organs out of her body.

Carolyn Dunnam was never revived before she died. If she'd been able to see what the monster armadillo had done to her body before her life ended, she'd have been EXTREMELY glad of that fact.

CHAPTER 22

Lisa found Toby's tent easily. He seemed to be the only one around though.

"Hey," she said on stepping out through the woods into the little clearing where the tent was pitched. Toby was propped up on a towel outside the tent, smoking crack.

"Wow, you really did come," Toby said on seeing her. "I'm so glad you could make it over."

"Yeah, everyone's gone searching for my little cousin's missing armadillo, so I thought I'd head over to see you instead."

"Cool, baby. Way to go," Toby said approvingly, then looked amused. "A missing armadillo?"

Lisa just nodded and shrugged. "Where's your girlfriend?" she asked cautiously. Even though she really wanted to be alone with him, she didn't want any drama.

"Alice?" Toby wagged a hand in the direction of the parking lot. "Oh, she went to town. Family emergency. She won't be back till tomorrow."

Hearing that guarantee of peace, Lisa sank down on the empty patch of beach towel that Toby indicated.

"What's that you're smoking?" she asked him. He was setting fire to something orange in there that she hadn't seen before.

"It's called Agent Orange. You might've heard about it. Crazy designer drug, makes just about everything else look like kid's play." He grinned at her. "Here, try some."

She pushed the hand proffering the crack pipe at her away. "Hey, man, ain't this the stuff that supposedly made that raccoon freak out and go on a killing spree?"

Toby laughed. "Oh, so you heard about that?"

"The ranger who killed it is a friend of my dad."

Toby's eyes widened at that revelation. "Wow, cool. That dude's like a local hero around here."

Then he fired up the pipe and took a hit. Afterward, he pushed the pipe toward Lisa again. "Go on, baby, take a hit. It'll beat your wildest expectations."

"I just don't wanna end up like that raccoon." She laughed, wanting desperately to indulge in the drug he was smoking, but at the same time, mindful of her father's repeated warnings about not intentionally messing up her mind.

"Relax, baby," Toby told her. "Orange doesn't hurt anyone that way. Not humans, anyway. You should know that. No one makes crack for raccoons to steal and sample. And even then, I think the damn coon got into a bad batch of the stuff."

Lisa nodded. "I ain't gonna get orange eyes like yours either?"

Toby nodded. "I already love you, baby. You don't miss a thing. You're smart like Alice wasn't—I mean, *isn't*." He looked serious. Hey, it takes a *long* time to get eyes like mine. Not for a couple months at least. Say, Lisa, where you from again?"

Texas."

"And you'll be around here for how long?"

"Just a week. Two weeks tops if the guys looking after my uncle's ranch don't screw things up down south."

Toby laughed. "So, girl, you ain't even gonna be here long enough to get eyes like mine. And even if you were, you might be immune to that effect; lots of folks are. And anyway, once you stop using, the orange tint vanishes anyway."

"Lisa laughed. "Fire up the pipe, man. Let's do it."

***

"So how do you like it?" Toby asked Lisa after she'd had a few hits of the drug.

"I've honestly no words," Lisa said, taking another hit of the orange fumes swirling up through the glass pipe and then handing it back to Toby. "My brain feels like . . ." It really felt like entire galaxies were being created inside her mind, like she would soon become a new person who was capable of anything she wanted to be.

"I know of a way to heighten the experience even more," Toby told her with a lust-filled glint in his eye.

Lisa nodded at him to hit her up again. "What way do you mean?"

Toby held the pipe to her lips and lit its end. "You ever had sex when you're cracked up?"

Lisa inhaled the fumes. Suddenly, in a rush of pumping blood and firing nerve synapses, her life seemed to begin anew. She'd tried coke once or twice with friends, but thrilling as it had been, that experience paled in comparison to this Agent Orange shit.

She giggled at Toby. "You don't waste any time, do you?"

"Never, when there's great drugs and a pretty girl available."

Lisa shook her head. "I've never even used crack before." Then, so that he didn't think she was lame and lose interest in her, she quickly added: "I've always wanted to, but you know . . . availability in our backwoods corner of Texas."

Toby nodded and moved closer to Lisa. "So, whatcha say, baby. Do you wanna fuck?"

Lisa thought about it for all of five seconds. She hadn't had sex in ages. "Yeah, why not? If it don't heighten the experience, we can always try it again." Then she remembered his girlfriend. "You sure Alice won't come back early?"

Toby fired up the crack pipe and took a long hit. "Forget Alice. We had a fight before she left. She might not come back ever."

He dropped the crack pipe on the blanket and then grabbed hold of Lisa's shoulders and began kissing her.

Then, the pair of them hurriedly undressed.

"Let's go inside," Toby said while peeling his shirt off.

But Lisa, who was down to just a bra and panties now, shook her head at him. "Fuck me here, man. I've always wanted to do it out in the open with just the sky above and the trees nearby.

"What if the ranger comes around?"

Lisa giggled. "I bet he'll watch us and jerk off."

So, they fucked outside there on the beach towel. Lisa discovered that Toby hadn't been lying. The Agent Orange did make sexual intercourse much more intense. Each thrust of his cock into her pussy seemed to penetrate down to a primitive part of her body, somewhere forgotten during evolution.

Strangely enough, even though she felt great fondness for him while they did it, she also experienced intense surges of inexplicable anger. At one point, she had the impression that she didn't want him inside of her body, that he was both taking advantage of her and raping her, and yet the next moment, she was pulling tightly on his buttocks, digging her nails in and moaning, "Deeper! Fuck me deeper!"

It was a thrilling ride, and soon, Lisa exploded in sexual ecstasy.

***

"So, how was that?" Toby asked Lisa after they'd cleaned up. Both of them were sitting on the beach towel, both still naked and passing the crack pipe between them. Even though Lisa Mitchell was completely new to Agent Orange and not yet an addict, she already understood how tempting the drug was. Staring down at the orange 'marshmallows' in the bag by Toby's side, she desired more of the pleasure they would give her.

Toby had said one could eat Agent Orange. Lisa reached a hand down into the bag and pulled out two of the chunks.

Toby frowned at her. "What the hell are you doing?"

She frowned back at him. "I'm gonna eat them. You said that works too."

"Hell no, you won't," Toby said angrily. "Give those back to me!" He tried snatching the chunks away from her, but she moved her hand out of the way.

"These ones are mine," she told him. "You've got the whole bag to yourself." She didn't know she was merely exhibiting the normal craving for more of the drug.

"Hey, man," she told him, getting up to her feet and pacing back and forth in front of the tent. "What's come over you all of a sudden? You were so cool before."

Toby got to his feet too. "Yeah, whatever, babe." Then his eyes lost their anger and he tried to explain: "See, I'm just worried 'bout running out of the stuff again, that's all. There was a whole lot more of it, but . . . hey, baby, what you looking at?"

Lisa was pointing behind Toby, at the creature that had walked around the side of the tent. Toby turned and looked at it, too. He gaped at the strange animal.

"Fuck, Lisa, ain't that the missing armadillo you said your family's out looking for?"

"I don't think so," Lisa stuttered in confusion. "It looks like Rocky, but Rocky was smaller in size—a lot smaller and . . . even if we leave out the fucked-up color of his eyes . . . he wasn't all covered in blood like that. And that looks like someone's hair stuck to his shell."

"No shit."

"And Rocky definitely didn't have all those evil-looking teeth," Lisa added when the armadillo opened his mouth. "Those teeth look sharp enough to bite through steel."

"Fucking run!" Toby yelled as the armadillo charged at them, snapping like an enraged lion.

Forgetting their clothes and everything in their panic, they ran off together. However, at this commencement of their flight a glaring difference was exhibited by both of them. Lisa, who wasn't yet addicted to Agent Orange, instinctively flung away the two chunks of the drug that she was holding.

Toby, on the other hand, who was a hardcore orangehead, first of all grabbed the bag of precious narcotics from off the towel before taking flight.

Toby and Lisa dashed through the woods, hurting their feet because they weren't wearing any shoes. Leaves and branches whipped their naked bodies.

When, after a while, it seemed like the mutant armadillo had stopped chasing them, they paused beside a tree.

"We need to locate Ranger Bentley fast," Toby told Lisa.

"Yeah, but we need to locate some clothes first," Lisa said, now instinctively covering her breasts with her hands, though there was no one nearby except Toby, whom she'd just had sex with.

"The ranger will know what to—shit! It's still following us! Go!"

With the crazed armadillo close behind, they took off running again.

Then Lisa tripped over something and crashed to the ground. Toby ran on for a short distance, then, realizing Lisa wasn't behind him, he turned back and saw her down in the underbrush.

He started back to help her up, but the crazy armadillo had already reached her.

And then the armadillo ran right past Lisa and kept coming after him. The armadillo was salivating now, as if it couldn't wait to sink its horrible teeth into him.

"What the fuck?" Forgetting Lisa, Toby turned and ran for his life.

While crashing through the bushes with the animal after him, Toby worked out what was happening:

That damn animal has orange eyes, meaning it's gotten addicted to Agent Orange, just like that raccoon did. And . . . hey, that means the armadillo is the one who stole our orange! And now he wants what I've got too. That's the reason why he didn't attack Lisa!

This understanding filled Toby with rage. His fright evaporated like water drying in a hot skillet.

Because of the depths of his crack addiction, Toby Miller didn't even consider throwing the desired Agent Orange to the crackhead animal to save his own life. That was completely out of the question.

This damn orange is mine and that animal won't take it from me. The hell it won't!

So, Toby stopped running and looked around for something to fight off the armadillo with.

He found a fallen branch that would make a suitable club. Holding the branch in one hand and the Agent Orange in the other, Toby waited like a gladiator for the armadillo to appear. He could hear it crashing through the trees towards him.

A part of his mind hoped that Lisa had escaped to call the ranger.

Then, the armadillo was charging out of the leaves at him. Suddenly, Toby realized he'd made a huge mistake waiting to fight with it. Armored up like it was, the thing seemed impervious. He couldn't figure out where to hit it to hurt it. He, on the other hand, was completely nude and thus completely exposed to bodily harm.

Maybe I should just let it have the fucking drug; I can always steal some more from Eddie Bush. Oh, hell no! This stash is mine! Over my dead body is anyone but myself using it.

The armadillo leapt at Toby. Toby swung his club at the armadillo and caught it flush on the shoulder. Instead of harming the animal, the wooden branch bounced out of Toby's grasp and then went spinning away over the armadillo's back into the trees.

Then the armadillo swiped at Toby with its claws, completely slitting his torso open from side to side.

Toby howled and then looked down at his belly. It now had six red openings across it. He could see his intestines. Stubbornly, however, he refused to let go of his precious drug, holding onto it even when the armadillo rammed into him like a tank, knocking him clean off of his feet and into a nearby tree.

Toby crashed to the ground, and the armadillo rushed over and slashed him again and again with its claws until he lay dead and unmoving amidst the grass and flowers.

***

With Toby's death, the package of Agent Orange finally spilled from his grasp. Rocky the armadillo quickly ripped the package open and started feasting on the drug.

Up till now, the armadillo had felt half-crazed by withdrawal symptoms. But now he felt like things were normal again.

Of course, eating the drug merely increased his craziness, but in a way that made sense to him. It made him feel like killing, but not 'killing' like he'd understood it before. Prior to his life-changing encounter with Agent Orange, Rocky had understood killing to be simply the right way to satisfy one's desire for food. But now, killing held an appeal all of its own. It was the right way to exert one's influence on the world. More importantly, it seemed nice to tear flesh open, to rip flesh from bone, and to break those bones too.

And now, too, food tasted better to the armadillo, possibly because humans tasted better than insects and worms.

After Rocky had eaten up all of the Agent Orange, he turned his attention to the dead man. He began eating parts of Toby's body. Part of this feeding was from hunger, and part of it was the armadillo's expression of rage towards Toby.

CHAPTER 23

Once Lisa had recovered from the sheer fright of falling down and thinking she was about to die, she got up again and tried to figure out where she was.

I'm fucking lost, she lamented as she stared down at the tree root that had tripped her up.

She wondered what had happened to Toby. Rocky . . . but that detail confused Lisa.

How the hell could that crazy animal be Rocky? But it has to be, they don't generally have armadillos in West Virginia, and it'd be too much of a coincidence to imagine someone else came vacationing in these same woods with their pet 'dillo.

Anyway Rocky (she assumed it was him for the moment) had charged off through the trees after Toby. And then she'd heard loud crashing about like they were fighting. And then she'd heard a howl.

Lisa hoped Toby was alright. But she didn't dare go check on him.

Uh uh, not me! I'm getting the hell away from here before Rocky comes back here to attack me! B-b-but . . . but where the hell am I?

That was the problem. There were trees around and trees overhead. She couldn't see the mountains because of the trees in the way, which meant she had no idea where the river was.

I need to get to a place where I can see either of those two landmarks. Then it'll be easy enough to find my way back to the family tent.

The one problem of course was that she wasn't wearing any clothes. She wondered how she was going to explain what had happened to them to her father.

I might be lucky and make it back to the campsite before daddy and Uncle Cody. Rendezvous time is noon. Actually, once I tell them Rocky is on the rampage in the woods, no one is gonna be overly concerned about my nakedness. I'll tell daddy I decided to go skinny dipping in the river and the crazy 'dillo startled me, so I left my clothes and ran for dear life.

She had no idea what the time was now. She'd not been wearing a watch, and in her terrified flight had left her cell phone over at Toby's tent.

Actually, my first order of business should be to get my phone from outside Toby's tent. My clothes are there too. Which leads me back to the initial problem of where the fuck am I? The ground here is perfectly level, which is no help at all. If it sloped upwards, I'd at least know which direction the mountains were.

Deciding that any direction was best so long as she soon reached a more sparsely forested area of the woods, Lisa set off walking.

I really, really hope Toby is fine, she thought as she walked off. *If Rocky hasn't killed him, we can both do that Agent Orange stuff together again. That shit is totally killer!*

***

After two minutes of walking and not making any real progress in working out her location, Lisa arrived at the hole in the ground.

She stared at the hole in fright.

The hole didn't scare her in itself. But there were two female human legs sticking out of the hole. Two female legs in blue jeans. She could tell the legs were female because the size of the sneakers at their ends were too small for a man to wear, and also because of the lady's purse that she now spotted a short distance away on the forest floor.

The woman's body was almost fully inside of the ground—just her shins and feet stuck out at about a forty-five degree angle. The sight was completely crazy; Lisa had never seen anything like it before.

Forgetting her own pressing troubles, Lisa ran over to the hole.

"Hey, are you okay?" she asked, tapping the woman's legs while making the enquiry. "Hey, are you okay?"

But she already suspected the woman wasn't okay at all. There was some blood on the nearby grass. Not a lot of blood, but enough to give the impression that the unknown woman was hurt, or hadn't willingly entered her present subterranean location. Lisa couldn't tell if the woman was dead or merely unconscious down there.

With no reply forthcoming, Lisa grabbed hold of the woman's feet and began dragging her out of the hole.

The woman emerged slowly, but not unwillingly. There was no resistance to Lisa's tugging, and Lisa soon had the woman's thighs and hips above ground as well.

And from that point onward, the horror of the situation came to light.

That the woman was dead became apparent once Lisa pulled the lower half of her torso out. No one could possibly survive not having any intestines inside of their body.

Lisa staggered off to be sick. On her way she noticed shreds of fabric strewn along the forest floor a short distance away. After vomiting to her gut's content (while throwing up it felt to her as if everything she'd eaten since arriving in West Virginia was leaving her body at once), she studied the scattered objects. She soon decided she was looking at the destroyed remains of a camper's backpack. The dead woman's intestines and a few other unrecognizable organs were tangled up in the mangled clothing and items, so she'd clearly been wearing it when she was attacked.

Rocky! Lisa thought in fright. *Rocky did this to her!*

With that understanding, and the sudden knowledge that she was very likely standing right beside one of the entrances to the now insanely mutated armadillo's burrow, Lisa felt major panic creeping up on her.

She looked over at the dead woman. The woman's arms and shoulders were still down out of sight and Lisa intended to leave them down there. Just looking at the dead woman nauseated her.

Then she looked around for the woman's cellphone.

Maybe I can call for help. Even with the screen locked, I'll still be able to make an emergency call!

She didn't find the cellphone. She did find the info in the woman's purse that her name was Carolyn Dunnam, and that she was a college student at WVU. In her ID photo, she looked young too, about Lisa's own age, which only heightened Lisa's sense of her own mortality.

Lisa dropped the purse and scowled at the trees around her.

Fuck, fuck, fuck, fuck, fuck!!! Where the hell can her cell phone be? I really need to call someone about all of this!

She stood there for a short while, frustrated and slowly growing angry. But then her fear of the rogue armadillo returned, and she hurriedly walked off through the bushes in a continuation of the direction in which she'd been headed.

But after walking just a short distance, she turned around and walked back to the dead woman.

Alright, I know this might be considered extremely ghoulish and all, but now that she's dead, she no longer needs her pants or sneakers. I, on the other hand, am very tired of walking around naked and barefoot.

Lisa now set herself the gruesome task of removing the corpse's still intact pants from her savaged body.

CHAPTER 24

It took Lisa a while to get the dead woman's pants off. This was mainly because she was so nervous about Rocky sneaking up on her while she was at it, that she forgot to pull the corpse's sneakers off first, and then wondered why the pants wouldn't come past her ankles. But once she realized her mistake, she quickly removed the shoes and then the pants.

She left the dead woman her underpants out of consideration for her modesty. Miss Dunnam had already been completely fucked up by Rocky; Lisa thought she at least deserved the dignity of not having her pussy exposed and inquisitive woodland creatures sniffing at it.

The pants fit Lisa perfectly. The sneakers were a little tight, but would do for this emergency.

And now that she had some clothes on again, Lisa decided to root through the shredded knapsack remains to see if there was anything else she could wear.

She wound up with most of a tee shirt. The tee shirt was bloody and ripped almost to shreds, but it beat wearing nothing over her breasts.

Then, relieved that Rocky still hadn't yet made an appearance, Lisa rushed off through the trees. Now that her feet and body were more protected, Lisa could move a lot faster. Soon, the trees thinned, and she saw the mountains.

Okay, so I was headed the wrong way, she thought as the trees parted yet further and she was able to get her bearings. *I need to adjust my direction again. If the mountains are over there, that means the river is that way and . . . time to turn left and . . .*

And that was when Lisa Mitchell tripped over something again, and once more fell down sprawling.

CHAPTER 25

Unaware that all hell was breaking loose a short distance away from him, Gary Bentley at last walked down to where the Mitchell family were camped.

He was surprised to find no one in camp. He stood there by the extinguished campfire and scratched his chin.

This is kinda weird. Hope nothing bad has happened to these folks.

Then he heard approaching footsteps. Next, he saw Slim Mitchell and the little kid.

"Hey, Uncle Ranger!" Jimmy shouted in delight on noticing him and ran over to him.

"How you doin', son?" Gary smiled and shook hands with the little boy. But he noticed that the kid looked glum afterward. "Hey, what's the matter with you, son?"

"His pet armadillo escaped," Slim Mitchell explained. "We've been looking for the darn thing all morning, but no sign of it yet."

Gary and Slim shook hands.

"But I thought that leash you had it on was secure," Gary said. "It looked mighty secure to me."

"Dunno how it happened," Slim said. "We all just woke up this morning and the 'dillo was gone."

"Do you know where he'll be, Uncle Ranger?" Jimmy asked. "I know Rocky. He's gonna be frightened where he is now."

Gary shook his head, then said, "No, son, I don't got no idea where he is. But you can rest assured that I won't stop lookin' for Rocky for you."

That seemed to calm the kid a little, and he walked off into the huge family tent.

"Can hardly stand on my feet at the moment," Slim said, lowering himself into one of the camping chairs. "How's your mornin' been, Gary?"

"Alright, alright. Nothing's happening. And that's exactly how I like it. Usually, when stuff happens in the woods, it's all bad. You know, forest fires and such like and folks littering everywhere." Then he frowned. "Hey, where's your daughter? Didn't you guys head off together?"

Slim shook his head. "We all split up to search for Rocky. I went with Jimmy and Cody went with Wendy. If Lisa ain't here, then she's still searching." He frowned. "Either that, or she's somewhere getting' high with those kids she met yesterday at the parking lot." Slim sighed. "And since she's clearly not here, I suspect it's the latter."

Gary laughed. "Ah, dude, there's kids for ya. First you want 'em, and then once you got 'em, particularly once they grow into their teens, you start wonderin' why you ever wanted 'em in the first place."

Both men laughed at that comment.

"How 'bout you, Gary? How many kids ya got?"

"One son. He's studying marine biology. Don't wanna be a forester like his dad here."

Slim thought about that for a while. "They never do wanna follow in their parent's footsteps, do they?"

Gary shook his head. "Not today's youth. I wanted to be just like my dad, and maybe you did too. But these kids of ours?"

They were silent for a while, two simple men pondering about their children, and then Slim asked: "Hey, man, you care for a cold beer? Day's just begun gettin' hot."

Gary shook his head again. "Nah, still workin'. Thanks for the offer tho'." He looked around the campsite and then down towards the river. "You guys enjoying yourself here?"

Slim nodded and lowered his voice. "Well, I had plans to, but that damn armadillo done gone and screwed up my day. Not to mention that my aching gut still hates Rocky with a passion." He laughed. "Don't tell the kid that tho'. He thinks Rocky and I are the best of friends now."

Gary laughed too. "Alright, man, gotta continue making my rounds. Tell Cody, I'll likely check on you guys again before I leave for home. Charlotte sends her regards."

"Okay, see ya later maybe."

"Yeah, and please remind the kid that I'll keep an eye out for his pet."

Gary walked off, feeling very amused.

CHAPTER 26

Lisa's fall stunned her and it took a while to get her wits around her again. But finally, she sat up and looked around to see what had tripped her. The forest floor had seemed clear enough.

Oh my God, not again.

Lisa was once more faced with the sight of a pair of feet sticking out of the ground. This set of feet was also female, and they had pink-painted toenails.

Fear gripped Lisa at the sight, causing her to instinctively scoot back on her ass till her back hit a tree, where she sat trembling, trying to figure out what was happening today in these woods.

This seems like one of those movies where a serial killer is killing young women and burying them in the forest.

Lisa was certain Rocky was responsible for this woman's death also. The fear that he might be nearby almost made her leap up and run off screaming her lungs out. But she somehow managed to control the panic that was attempting to take her over.

Then she moved closer to the corpse and examined what she could see of it.

It occurred to her that maybe her thoughts about a serial killer roaming the woods weren't too far off the truth. Unlike the other dead woman, this one hadn't been pulled or pushed into a hole. Actually, she wasn't buried deep at all. The reason her feet were above ground was because her grave was a shallow one, mostly just soil piled over her body. It seemed her killer hadn't had the right tools to dig up the earth, and so had contented himself with making a shallow trench in the ground and humping soil over it. He seemed to have been distracted as well because he'd neither chosen a good spot for the grave, like somewhere under the trees where no one would notice it for ages, nor had he even bothered to heap branches, undergrowth, or even leaves on the grave in an attempt to disguise it.

Lisa was suddenly curious to see who was buried there. She was certain now that Rocky wasn't the killer, which reduced her fear and increased her urge to dig this unknown woman up.

Using her hands to scoop the soil off, she began at the end opposite the corpse's feet. The soil parted easily and Lisa was soon revealing a woman's face. She worked faster now, horrified, but also unable to stop working, as if the corpse was demanding that she reveal its identity to the world.

Then, when Lisa had cleared all of the sand away from the dead woman's face, she stared at it in additional horror.

Hey, this is Toby's girlfriend Alice! It's her! I'm sure it's her! She didn't leave for home like he said. Toby killed her! He killed her!

Lisa's suppressed panic threatened to return multiplied. The shock of unexpectedly finding Alice dead like this threatened to unnerve her. And it might have succeeded in doing so if she'd not then heard a loud noise approaching her through the forest.

Lisa had no doubt that whatever was making the racket was heading for her. She was the only one out here, if one excluded the corpse, of course. But who could possibly want anything to do with a corpse?

Rocky's found me! she thought in an intense panic now. Leaping to her feet, she ran away from the corpse and hid behind the thick trunk of a nearby oak.

She got into concealment just in time. A moment after she ducked behind the oak tree, Rocky, now doubly covered in gore, charged out of the forest.

The mutated armadillo ran straight up to Alice's partially exposed corpse and stopped.

Lisa watched, her knuckles in her mouth, her legs trembling. Her entire body felt boneless as jelly. She clenched her legs tight, both to prevent her knees from knocking together and also to keep from pissing herself.

Oh my God! If he notices that I'm here! Shit, shit, shit! 'Dillos don't see too great, but they have a great sense of smell.

But that was the odd thing. Rocky now made no attempt to sniff Lisa out. Instead, the armadillo began properly unearthing Alice's corpse.

The armadillo worked around the body in a nonviolent and methodical way, scraping the sand off of Alice's body just like Lisa had done, but much more efficiently seeing as its claws were specifically designed for that task.

Watching Rocky's strange behavior, Lisa's panic reduced.

Alright, so he's not here after me. So, what's he after then?

This was soon revealed. Once Alice's body was completely free of dirt, Rocky began sniffing it up and down, once more in the same methodical style he'd used while unearthing it. Then, once the armadillo had finished sniffing up and down Alice's body, he used his front claws to slit her pants open.

Hell no, he ain't gonna fuck her corpse, is he?

The thought completely revolted Lisa, and she was pleased to discover that such wouldn't be the case here.

What did happen was that once Rocky had opened up Alice's pants, he stripped the fabric aside to reveal her pockets, which even from concealment, Lisa could see, bulged out. Then the armadillo slit open both pockets to reveal packages of Agent Orange.

***

The late Toby Miller was right to suspect that there had originally been more Agent Orange in their tent.

Ever since they'd arrived at the camp, his equally late girlfriend Alice Brown had been stealing bags of Agent Orange from their stash.

But since, with the normal orangehead's lack of proper reasoning, Alice had been unable to figure out where to keep the filched drugs, she'd finally decided to keep them on her person.

This was safe enough since she and Toby hardly ever had sex anymore. Two other missing packages of Agent Orange were hidden inside Alice's bra, one on either side.

The titillating location of these two latter packages (which Rocky the armadillo would soon expose also) had worried Alice that Toby might find them since they made her quite-small breasts look much bigger.

***

Lisa settled down to watch Rocky eat the Agent Orange he'd recovered from Alice's body.

Even though she'd only sampled the strange orange narcotic that one time with Toby, Lisa strongly felt the waste of the drug as the armadillo ate it all up. She imagined the incredible high those orange chunks Rocky was so carelessly (and greedily) scarfing down could provide her, and only some modicum of self-preservation instinct in a distant corner of her brain prevented her from charging the animal and demanding her share of the potent and precious drug.

But thankfully, common sense prevailed, and she didn't commit suicide. Still, she felt very offended by the waste as the animal ate up all of the drug.

Lisa began thinking it would be a very good idea to kill Rocky. Otherwise, the greedy beast might eat up all of the Agent Orange in existence.

CHAPTER 27

At around the same time that Lisa was trying to work out an effective way to kill Rocky, the crackhead armadillo, Gary Bentley strode into Toby and Alice's campsite.

The campsite was, of course, empty. Gary was puzzled by the coincidence.

Second empty campsite I've visited today. Maybe these folks are off looking for their runaway chimpanzee or something else exotic like that.

"Hey, I'm Ranger Gary Bentley! I'm just checking in to see if you folks are alright!"

No reply. Gary repeated the call and frowned at the silence.

Yeah, there didn't have to be any criminal reason why a campsite would be deserted like this. But something in this case seemed off.

All these clothes on the ground as if . . . as if the couple decided to hell with the tent, let's do it out in the open. Alright, so what next? Did they both decide to go take a dump at the same time? And if they are both emptying their bowels in the woods, why the hell would the woman—'cos that's a woman's cellphone for sure, with that pink protective casing—why would she leave her cell phone behind here on the forest floor? Women tend to even take their phones into the shower with 'em.

Suddenly worried, Gary opened up the tent flap and peeked inside. He'd have been relieved to stumble on two naked people and have them call him a peeper, but there was nobody around. The tent also looked like any normal camping tent; there was no sign of a struggle.

Gary paced around the campsite for a bit, trying to make up his mind as to whether something bad had happened here or not.

Finally, he figured he'd wait here a little longer to see if the couple who owned this tent came back. If not, he'd call it into the ranger station.

If they need looking for, better we start looking for 'em early, while we got the aid of daylight.

Then Gary noticed something that looked disturbingly familiar hidden in the grass.

Oh no, it can't be, he told himself as he walked over there and picked the object up.

Oh, no, it can't be, he told himself again, as he realized that it definitely was what he was trying to deny it being.

It might just be orange candy, he reasoned, as he lifted the little orange 'marshmallow' to his lips and took a tentative lick at it. But Gary Bentley knew that taste alright. What he'd just found here in the grass was the dreaded Agent Orange. The drug of his waking nightmares.

Gary spat several times, fearing contamination by even the tiny amount on the tip of his tongue. Then, as he straightened up again, he noticed a second chunk of Agent Orange near a bush. He picked it up and sighed.

The gift that just can't stop giving, he thought dourly. *Can't stop giving me trouble, that is, and looks like it's back to gift me some more.*

Rolling the Agent Orange nuggets in his palm, Gary stood there thinking for a while. Since he'd seen that first chunk of orange narcotic lying there in the grass, something had been bothering him.

Each time we've had Agent Orange trouble in these here woods, it's been animal trouble. Every single time there's been some animals involved. Including several that shouldn't have been here in the first place, like that damn crocodile and the cockroaches from hell. And now, Charlotte's cousin's family the Mitchells have lost their pet armadillo, another animal that shouldn't be in these woods anyway to begin with. And if my past bad karma is anything to go by . . .

Gary sighed and slipped both chunks of Agent Orange into his shirt pocket.

. . . I'd better find that missing armadillo before it finds any of this drug. Or else there'll be serious hell to pay in these woods.

He gave the empty tent yet another puzzled look. *Where the hell did these two dumb drug addicts go? Have they been killed by drug dealers, or what? This is looking mighty bad already.*

Gary looked down at the pistol holstered at his hip.

Armadillos have hard shells. I remember what happened to Slim Mitchell when he tried shooting that missing armadillo, and that was before it had eaten any Agent Orange, which I'm hoping it hasn't, but I can't take any chances on that.

He shook his head. *Nah, this sidearm won't do the job today. I'd better go get my shotgun from the ranger truck.*

Now alarmed, Gary Bentley set off at a run for the Sleepaway Campground's parking lot.

CHAPTER 28

It soon occurred to Lisa Mitchell how dumb she was being, standing here watching Rocky eat crack cocaine when she should be making her way to safety.

Am I really thinking of killing it? How? The damn animal is armor-plated. Now it's looking like a tank that's come to life.

She didn't know how it could be possible, but while she'd been watching Rocky eat, she thought she'd noticed additional changes to his body as he lay there, with his body half on and half off of Alice's corpse.

His eyes had become even 'oranger' than before and stuck out even more from the sides of his head. His head had become more pointed, his tail thicker. And he seemed more armored than previously. Worst of all, his legs looked thicker and stronger, and his claws seemed much more deadly.

Now is definitely the time when I should be getting out of here. I now know exactly where I am. I'm about a hundred yards away from Toby's campsite. Which means I'm not that far away from the camping trail.

Right when she thought that, she imagined she could hear someone running past in the near distance, though they were still out of sight.

Lisa began stepping backward from her hiding place behind the oak tree. She'd just placed her left foot softly down on the ground behind her when Rocky took a huge bite out of Alice's thigh.

The sight of Rocky's doing so startled her so much that she leapt back in fright and landed on a large twig that snapped with a loud noise.

Rocky, who'd been swallowing the flesh he'd ripped off of Alice's leg, instantly spat it out and leapt to his feet.

Lisa turned and ran. She didn't wait to see if Rocky was coming after her or not. She ran till she found a tree in the way, changed direction, and ran farther. The camping trail she'd expected to find eluded her.

Finally, she stopped.

Fuck! I can't believe I've gotten lost again. No, I'm not lost—I can still see the mountains. I just got turned around in my panic, and I'm now further into the woods than I was before. Thank heavens, I seem to have lost that killer 'dillo too. Now, I just need to remain calm and make my way over to Toby's tent and get my cell phone.

Lisa kept going, every now and then, looking around her to make sure Rocky wasn't shadowing her.

Oh my God, I can't believe I fucked Toby! And after he killed his girlfriend! What a douchebag!

And then Lisa stepped out from behind a group of trees and discovered that somehow or another she'd been walking around in circles. Suddenly, she was right back at the hole in the ground with the dead woman partly inside of it.

Carolyn Dunnam's corpse lay exactly how Lisa had left her, mostly out of the hole and with the visible part of her torso shredded and emptied of all organs. And as expected, her lower half wore just panties now.

The corpse's naked legs seemed to accuse Lisa of grave robbery.

Lisa ignored the revisited madness of the scene in favor of her confusion.

What? I can't believe it. How in the hell did I wind up here again? How could I get turned around so badly?

And she now realized that she wasn't alone here either. Over on her left, Rocky was emerging from a similarly large hole in the ground. The armadillo shot out of the hole at speed, reaching Lisa before she even had a chance to turn around and face him.

Rocky rammed into Lisa and she felt a horrible pain in her side and then she crashed to the ground. She rolled over and managed to stand up but then realized that she was bleeding profusely from where the armadillo had hit her.

She looked down at herself. Owing to the tattered state of her borrowed tee shirt, Lisa couldn't immediately assess the damage to her body. But when she did, she screamed. Half of the flesh on the left side of her torso was visibly peeling away, some of it sliced clean off of her ribs. Red liquid was jetting out of her side and she was already feeling woozy from blood loss.

She heard a sound behind her and managed to turn around.

The last thing Lisa Mitchell saw was Rocky the armadillo leaping through the air at her, with his claws slicing at her face.

Lisa screamed again, this time from dire agony as death met her head-on.

Then she crashed to the forest floor with half of her face peeled off, her brain sliced completely in half, and her left arm almost completely ripped out of its socket.

Lisa was dead on arrival at the ground.

CHAPTER 29

As Gary was getting his shotgun out of his pickup truck, he thought he heard a scream.

He paused in what he was doing and listened. When the noise didn't repeat, Gary relaxed, but only slightly. Still, he waited, waited patiently to see if he heard it again.

Then he sighed. *I'm getting really jumpy now. Like I'm hearin' things. That noise—yes, it did sound like a woman screaming, but really it could've been anything.*

The sound had come from the direction of the Lake Placid Trailer Park. Once Gary had gotten out his shotgun and locked up the pickup truck again, he stood beside the truck and stared in the direction of the trailer park. He wasn't being overly concerned; he'd had massive trouble over at that trailer park before.

And the damn park ain't even in my jurisdiction.

"Hey, ranger, what's with the shotgun? You got trouble in the woods?"

Gary turned around. The speaker was a fat young kid in his late teens, who had a suspicious-smelling cigarette in his mouth. He was in the company of two other youths, a girl and a boy in the same age range.

"Nothing you guys gotta bother yourselves about," Gary replied. "Just some bear trouble around the trailer park. Shotgun's just in case."

The kids nodded and turned to walk away. Then, a thought occurred to Gary.

"Hey, guys, you didn't happen to hear something like someone screaming just now, did ya?"

The two young men shook their heads, but their female companion looked surprised.

"I thought that was just the wind I heard just now," she said. She looked curiously at Gary. "Oh, so you heard it too?"

Gary nodded at her. "I really hope *it was* just the wind," he said and then took off running before they could question him further.

CHAPTER 30

While searching for Rocky the armadillo, Cody Mitchell and Wendy had walked all the way along the river to Lake Placid. There, they'd enquired of the locals if they'd noticed a stray armadillo walking about. The fishermen they'd asked had found their story very amusing, and had found Cody and Wendy's ten-gallon hats even more amusing, but no one had seen Rocky.

And so, after sitting on a pier and enjoying the scenery for a while, Cody and Wendy started back along the river again.

"Don't know bout you, honey," Cody said after a while, "but I definitely need a breather after all this walking. So far we must've covered five or six miles in our search for that damn 'dillo." He sighed. "For a guy supposed to be on vacation, I sure am doin' a lot of walking."

Wendy shrugged. "Well, it was your idea to bring the animal along on the trip."

Cody shook his head and stopped walking. "Not mine, love, Jimmy's."

Wendy fanned her pretty face with her cowboy hat. "You could've said no to him. Cody, you're spoiling that boy something fierce. He's got you wrapped around his li'l fingers."

"Alright, let's not argue 'bout it," Cody grunted and sat down. "What's done is done. I just hope we do find the damn 'dillo, or the kid's gonna make our lives miserable all the while that we're here."

Wendy rolled her eyes at that thought, and sat down too.

She and Cody had stopped at a point where the river flowed through a rocky channel and almost became a shallow pool. Farther inland, where they sat now, was nice and grassy, and the trees here gave comfortable shade in the heat of the day.

"One could actually fall asleep here," Cody told Wendy, draping an arm around her shoulder.

"Yeah, except that we're all supposed to rendezvous at the tent by noon." She looked at her watch. "And, Cody, noon was fifteen minutes ago. Honey, what're we gonna do?"

"We ain't doing nothing," Cody said. "We've just missed the appointment, that's all." He sighed. "At least that puts off seeing Jimmy's disappointment when we tell him our search was fruitless."

"Maybe I can call the others at the tent," Wendy said, getting out her cell phone. "Oh, doggone it—still no service." She frowned at Cody. "How 'bout yours, sweetie. You got any bars?"

Cody didn't even bother getting his phone out of his pocket. "Hon, we both use Verizon. If you ain't got bars, then I ain't got none either."

Cody Mitchell then stretched himself out comfortably on the grass. "Honey, I'm just gonna take a nap, right now. Join me if you like, or go for a swim."

"A swim? You can't be serious. There's . . ."

"Exactly, honey, there's *no one* around, just us and all these trees, who ain't wearin' any clothes either." He grinned lasciviously. "So, take your ass off for a swim, and when you're nice and wet and nekkid, come wake me up and give me some lovin'." He gestured westward. "Don't worry 'bout the kid. Jimmy's with Slim; those two will be okay. Lisa, too, should be back at the camp by now."

Still grinning, Cody Mitchell then covered his face with his hat and went to sleep.

CHAPTER 31

Wendy Hearst sat beside Cody for a short while after he'd dozed off, wondering how soon it would be before he got up the nerve to ask her to marry him.

We've been dating for two years now, and he's still scared I'm gonna die on him like his ex-wife did. All I can do in the meantime is love this good man and keep trying to make him forget that nasty experience.

So far, it looked like she was succeeding. *Jimmy already loves me and wants me to be his new momma. He's told me so himself. But his daddy here . . .*

With a sigh of frustrated desire, Wendy got to her feet.

Might as well go have that swim Cody suggested. He's right, this is a great place, no one around 'cept us and the trees.

She stripped down to her underwear, walked down to the river's edge, and slipped into the water.

The water was deliciously cool against her skin, and just like her cousin's husband, Ranger Bentley had told them about the area where they'd set up their camp, this was also one of those places where one could see right down to the bottom of the river. It wasn't deep here, just about eight feet or so, and when Wendy dove below the river surface, she felt very amused at the way the little fish scattered at her coming.

Wendy was a good swimmer, if a little out of practice. With a powerful breaststroke, she swam halfway across to the opposite bank and then back again.

And it was when she was returning that she noticed a strange thing underwater. When she dipped her head in the water between strokes, she imagined she saw Rocky the armadillo down there.

Nah, that's impossible, Wendy thought. But still, she paused her forward movement and trod water. But then, deciding it made good sense to investigate, just in case that really was their missing armadillo down there on the river's bottom, she took a deep breath and dove beneath the river's surface.

Now that Wendy was fully underwater, she had a clearer view.

Well, I'll be damned, she thought in surprise. *It really is Rocky. But what the hell is the 'dillo dragging about down there?*

She went up again for air, took a deep breath of it, and resubmerged.

This time, Wendy went right down to the bottom. And the closer she got to Rocky, the weirder what she saw became.

No, maybe this ain't Rocky. This clearly is an armadillo walking across the riverbed tho'—yeah, they can do that for a short distance, five or six minutes I think . . . but what the hell is it draggin' along like that?

The unknown object had gotten tangled up in water weeds. Now, just before Wendy would need to surface to breathe again, the object the strange armadillo was dragging pulled free of the weeds. On seeing what it was, Wendy almost forgot to hold her breath. The need to scream in horror, to scream for help, almost overwhelmed her.

The armadillo was pulling Lisa Mitchell's severed head along the rocky riverbed, dragging it by her long blonde hair. Rocky wasn't heading for the opposite riverbank, but down towards the Lake Placid end of the river. Now that it was free of the water weeds, the severed head rose upward in the sluggish current, like it was a kite.

It was upside down, but clearly recognizable.

Yeah, yeah, yeah, it is her! Wendy thought as she kicked for the surface. *Her head's split open like a Halloween pumpkin, and half of her face is missing, but that's her hair and her mouth, and those are definitely the earrings she was wearing this morning. Oh my God!*

These were the frightened thoughts that raced through Wendy's mind as her head broke the water's surface, when her single thought switched to the need to reach the riverbank and wake Cody up.

So, Wendy swam, but then she felt something snare her by the right ankle. She felt horrible pain in that foot, as if it was being bitten off.

She screamed, but it was really only a half-scream, because she was already being pulled underwater when she made it, and water filled her mouth before the sound was completed.

Then she, too, was down on the riverbed, being held in place by the armadillo's weight as he pulled on her right foot. She tried to rise, but the armadillo's body was like an anchor. Now that he had her, he had dug his claws into cracks in the river bed and was holding on tight. His teeth were clamped tightly into her ankle, and though she beat at his head with her fists, he just wouldn't let go. Her blood spilled from her punctured foot, and bubbles of precious air spilled from her lips.

She looked overhead at the sky above the water and wondered how to save herself.

Stick my fingers in his eyes! she thought in desperation as she felt her air beginning to run out. *Jab him in the eyes! My long fingernails are sure to do some damage!*

She attempted to do this, folding her body double to reach down where the armadillo was, and then swiping at the monstrous creature's head.

Had they both been above ground, this tactic would surely have saved Wendy's life. But underwater, her arm moved sluggishly towards its target, and the armadillo (Wendy no longer believed this strangely mutated thing was the family pet) easily evaded her swinging arm and swiped at her with his front claws.

Wendy never worked out, which surprised her more, the pain of the armadillo's claws stabbing through her throat, or how sharp they seemed to be—the claws felt like knives going through her body.

Now, she was doubly held in place, because the demonic creature with the horrible orange eyes refused to withdraw his claws from her neck.

Wendy gasped and pissed herself in the water and bled to death down there, with the armadillo refusing to let go of her, until her body completely stopped resisting his assault.

CHAPTER 32

When Cody Mitchell awoke a short while later, he was surprised that he couldn't find Wendy anywhere.

Where the hell has the woman gotten to now? he wondered after noticing the neat pile that she'd made of her clothes and shoes, cell phone, and hat by his side.

Then he decided that maybe she'd gone off into the bushes to piss or shit. Which also made little sense to him, since, seeing as he'd been asleep, she could have done either of those nearby without bothering him in the least.

So, he sat and waited for her to return. Ten minutes later, however, she still hadn't returned.

Cody now became worried. In addition to the fact that he didn't know where Wendy was, the ground around him had just begun rumbling. It wasn't anything serious, but felt a lot like someone was blasting rock in a mine nearby. He didn't pay it no mind, however, what with West Virginia being a mining state and all.

But where's Wendy?

Cody got to his feet and walked down to the water's edge. The sun was still almost directly above and so it took him a little while to work out what he was looking at down there in the shimmering river water.

Oh no!

He could see Wendy underwater. She was upside down, with her hair either stuck between rocks or entangled in a clump of weeds so that she couldn't float up to the surface. Cody didn't know whether his girlfriend had drowned or had been attacked by a shark because her body was all slashed up, with her arms and legs opened up like sausage skins and her intestines rolling about in the sluggish current like cooking spaghetti. In keeping with the slow progress of the river at this point, faint trails of red dribbled from her wounds into the water.

But that wasn't all. Right beside Wendy's body, Cody could clearly make out a severed human head. He didn't know whose head it could possibly be, but it looked to have been savaged as brutally as Wendy's body.

By now, Cody Mitchell was trembling with horror. He couldn't help it. Seeing the woman he loved (and was getting ready to propose marriage to) ripped up like a shark had taken out its grudge against humans on her was beyond his comprehension.

And I wish those miners would stop their damn blasting. I need to fucking think, and I can't think when the ground keeps shaking like we're bombing Iraq again.

Cody couldn't work out what to do first. *Should I run to get help, or do I try to get Wendy's corpse out of the water? And—oh God—who the hell's that down there with her? That head. Oh, God, please don't let it be Lisa!*

Cody finally decided to go for help. This made sense to him because Wendy was already dead. *I can't save her anymore. And unless the cops see this for themselves, it's gonna be hard as hell to believe!*

By now, tears were streaming down Cody's face. He turned and hurried away from the water's edge. He got out his cell phone to see if possibly he could make a call. And then the ground vibrated under his feet again.

This time, the rumbling was so intense that Cody went flying through the air. He landed hard and sat up cussing:

"Damn those God-damned miners! I should fucking sue—!"

But then he realized that it couldn't have been miners making the ground rumble like this, because . . .

Because I ain't been hearing any explosions. And besides, this last time I heard noise UNDERNEATH me!

But Cody couldn't hang around to figure out this oddity. He had his dead girlfriend to consider. The earth's rumbling had merely been a brief interlude in his sadness, a minor punctuation mark between bursts of grief, the well of which it appeared might never run dry.

Cody leapt up to his feet and hurried off towards the forest.

Then he stepped right into a hole in the ground that hadn't been there five minutes ago. Yes, he'd walked right over this very same spot five minutes ago, and the ground had been solid.

This too was only a partial observation, because falling into the hole like that had snapped Cody Mitchell's ankle. He'd heard it break as his left foot landed down there with the corresponding pain rocketing up his leg.

Dammit! Cody sat there on the forest floor in confusion. His heart was pounding now, both from fright and sorrow, and pain and adrenaline. He pulled his foot out of the ground and winced. His left foot was bent outwards at a right angle to his leg. He wouldn't be going anywhere now.

All Cody could do was drag himself away from the hole and pray that help would come. And quickly at that.

"Hey, is there anyone nearby? Can anyone hear me!?" he shouted. "I'm wounded, and I need a doctor! And my girlfriend is dead too! Hey, can anyone hear me!?"

But it seemed no one could. He heard no replies. Cody tried calling for help on his phone. But phone service was just as dead as before.

And the ground was still rumbling. Now that the wounded man had realized that there weren't any mining or construction companies blasting holes in the nearby countryside, the strange vibrations underground were taking on a frightful significance to him. He couldn't not connect it to the state in which Wendy's body hung in the water, all shredded up and bleeding from lots of wounds.

I'm startin' to REALLY believe Charlotte's tale 'bout that crack-addicted coon
. . .

"What the hell? Rocky? Is it you?"

The animal had popped up so suddenly from the ground that it might have teleported itself down to earth.

Cody gaped.

For certain, this had to be missing little Rocky. But first off, this creature wasn't little anymore and . . . now it was coming directly at Cody with a murderous grin on its face and clearly-projected craziness in its crazy orange eyes.

Cody forgot his ankle was broken and tried to get up and run.

Yelling in agony, he crashed down to the ground again.

Shit!

Biting his tongue to control the pain, he began scooting back on his ass to get away from the monster that he'd once known as a pet. But it kept pace with him easily and when finally, it leapt on him, he discovered it had simply been waiting for him to unknowingly back himself up against a tree, which he'd just done.

Cody screamed and screamed again as Rocky began tunneling into his body, spraying his intestines and other internal organs all over the forest floor.

By the time the armadillo was done, Cody Mitchell lay in close to a hundred bleeding pieces. Meat, bone, brains, guts, eyes, hair; everything shredded and discarded with unrelenting anger.

After eating some of those pieces of Cody Mitchell, the murderous mutated crackhead armadillo walked off through the forest again.

CHAPTER 33

Slim and Jimmy Mitchell were sitting watching the river.

"I sure hope Dad and Miss Wendy find Rocky," Jimmy told his uncle.

"Me too, son," Slim replied. Then he got a serious look on his face. "But, Jimmy, I really don't know what's taking them all so long to get back here." He looked at his watch. "See for yourself, Jimmy. We was supposed to meet up here an hour ago."

Jimmy nodded. "Even Cousin Lisa ain't back yet, Uncle Slim."

Slim nodded. "Yeah, though in your cousin's case I may have an idea why she ain't come home yet. I just hope she—"

"Hey, it's Rocky!" Jimmy interrupted Slim with a delighted scream. "Uncle Slim, Rocky's come back to us!"

Slim stared at the armadillo that was walking towards the camp from downriver. He immediately saw that something was wrong with Rocky. In addition to his body looking oddly distorted, the armadillo was covered in blood and had strips of denim fabric stuck to his shell.

Little Jimmy, however, was already getting up and walking over to go greet his pet. "Hey, Rocky, why'd you run off on us like that? Hey, what happened to your eyes? And you're bleeding—"

"Hey, son, I think it's time to leave," Slim said and snatched Jimmy out of the way, right as Rocky charged at him.

The armadillo missed hitting Jimmy by a hair and crashed into the family tent instead. By then, Slim was already running for safety with Jimmy in his arms.

Once they'd attained some high ground, at a good distance from the river, Slim put Jimmy down. By now, the place where he'd been shot was hurting him like hell, and he couldn't have carried the kid another yard.

He and Jimmy watched from relative safety, while Rocky completely trashed their campsite, running back and forth through the Mitchell family's tent until all that remained was its frame. And then the armadillo began chopping at the frame with his claws, biting at it with his teeth, and smashing it with his tail. Finally, the tent itself collapsed on top of Rocky, who immediately re-emerged from a hole he ripped out in its top and continued his destruction of the tent's remains and the sundry camping gear it had contained.

"Hey, why's Rocky behavin' like that, Uncle Slim?" Jimmy asked in confusion. "He's tearing everything up like he's mad at our family. I don't understand it, Uncle Slim. Rocky used to be so gentle and nice."

Slim nodded. "Oh, he's mad all right. But I don't think it's our family that's his problem." He looked down at Jimmy and gestured in the general direction of the parking lot. "We both need to find Ranger Bentley ASAP."

They hurried off.

CHAPTER 34

Try hard as he might, Gary Bentley didn't find the distressed woman he'd heard screaming. And so, at last he gave up the search.

I should be relieved that I can't find her, 'cos that means nothing's wrong. But I don't think that's the case. My ranger instincts keep telling me that if I keep searching, I'm gonna find something really horrible waiting for me around here. But at the moment, I simply don't have the time to keep looking for it.

He patted the two chunks of Agent Orange in his shirt pocket.

I gotta go search for that damn armadillo before it finds any of this evil drug and eats it.

With a seemingly almost impenetrable wall of greenery facing him, Gary Bentley didn't know he was standing barely a yard away from Lisa Mitchell's now-headless corpse, and that a short distance away from her body lay another half-naked female corpse that had been shoved into a hole.

(The puzzle of how Lisa Mitchell came to be wearing the other dead girl's pants and shoes would be solved by the WV police in a week's time.)

And so, none the wiser that he was barely five yards from the disaster he was(n't) looking for, Gary Bentley walked off in the opposite direction.

CHAPTER 35

As fate would have it, shortly after Gary Bentley left that area of the forest, Slim and Jimmy Mitchell walked right into it.

Just like Slim's daughter Lisa had done earlier, the pair had gotten lost too.

After walking for a while, Slim called a halt. "I thought we was headed the right way," he told Jimmy. "But I think we're lost."

"What are we gonna do, Uncle?" Jimmy asked.

Slim frowned. "I dunno, son." He leaned against a tree and scratched his chin. "I suppose the best thing for us to do would be to just walk back the way we came." He pointed. "Straight over that way. Then, when we reach the point we started out from, we can try again."

His phone beeped then, with a cascade of sounds as a lot of email message notifications came in.

Slim cracked a smile. "Well, I'll be damned." He nodded to his nephew. "Hey, Jimmy, we got a phone signal over here. I'm gonna try and call your dad. Look around if you wanna, but don't wander off where you won't hear me callin' you. And please, please watch out for that darn pet of yours. That 'dillo's crazy now. You saw for yourself how he was tearin' up our tent somethin' crazy, an' I don't wanna have to explain to my kid brother how I let Rocky bite ya to death, or something nasty like that."

Jimmy nodded. "Alright, Uncle Slim," and walked off.

Slim dialed his brother's number. He got no reply and then left a voicemail. He didn't have Wendy's number, but he of course had Lisa's. So, he called Lisa. Same result. He left Lisa a voicemail too.

How the hell is it that the phone works fine around here and nowhere else? Slim grumbled to himself.

And then he heard Jimmy scream. "Uncle Slim! Uncle Slim, come quick!"

The boy sounded deathly frightened and so Slim Mitchell immediately set off running towards the sound of his voice. Jimmy had walked out of sight and so Slim had to run through thick foliage for a short distance, before he located him.

"Hey, Uncle Slim, where are you!?" Jimmy called again. "Come quickly!"

Slim had already arrived by the boy's side. "What the heck is going on over here?"

Jimmy pointed down at a body a short distance away from them. A young woman's body by the looks of it.

"I think it's Cousin Lisa," the young boy said, and began weeping. "She's dead!"

"What? What you mean, son!?" Slim hurried over and crouched by the corpse, wincing when he saw that it was headless. Its lack of a head made identification difficult, but the corpse most definitely had Lisa's hands and arms.

Slim almost passed out from the shock of it.

"Lisa! Who the hell did this to her?"

"There's another body over there, Uncle Slim," Jimmy told him, pointing while wiping the tears from his eyes.

"What?" With his mind still reeling from the sight of his dead daughter, Slim Mitchell got to his feet and walked over to have a look. Jimmy stayed behind, like he didn't want a second look at the dead body.

This second corpse was in an even worse state than Lisa's, with its upper half all ripped up into shreds . . .

Ripped up in exactly the same way that that damned 'dillo was tearing up our campsite a short while ago. Slim turned and looked in horror at his daughter's corpse.

You mean that sonofabitch armadillo killed Lisa? Rocky killed Lisa? Slim started to become enraged. *Oh, I'm gonna make that 'dillo pay! I'm gonna catch it and roast it for dinner. Yeah, I'm gonna—*

But then he saw the armadillo in question charging out of the woods.

Once again Rocky was running at Jimmy, with the unmistakable intention of killing him.

With anger in his heart, Slim Mitchell hurled himself at Rocky.

Once again, he was just in time, slamming into the crazy armadillo right before he'd have hit Jimmy.

"Run, son!" Slim shouted as he and Rocky went down in a tangle. "Save yourself. Get the hell away from here!"

Jimmy took off running.

CHAPTER 36

The battle between Slim Mitchell and Rocky the Crackhead Armadillo was brief and brutal.

Slim couldn't win, and he knew this. Slamming into Rocky like he'd done seemed to have immediately undone all of the stitches the doctors had put into him after he'd gotten shot.

Once Rocky concentrated on attacking Slim, he could hardly mount any defense. The armadillo's shell was too hard to penetrate and his claws now seemed as long as the heads of scythes. The claws were apparently as sharp as scythes too, Slim discovered when the little monster began slashing at him with them.

But Slim intended to get a measure of revenge for Lisa's death. *If this 'dillo is gonna die, I'm most certainly gonna have a hand in its death. Nobody, and I mean, fucking nobody, does that to my Lisa and gets away with it!*

So, while Rocky stabbed at him and slashed him, Slim reached up to the side of the armadillo's head, grabbed one of his swollen 'lightbulb' eyes, and pulled on it with all of his might.

The eyeball that Slim pulled—the left one—first popped out of Rocky's head and then exploded into orange and yellow goop.

Rocky screamed in pain.

Score one for me! Slim thought, reaching for Rocky's other eye.

But before he could dish out similar treatment to that eye also, the armadillo slashed him in the face too, completely blinding him and ending what had really been a one-way conflict from the get-go.

Fuck you, 'dillo piece of shit! Slim Mitchell thought and slumped down on the grass and died.

CHAPTER 37

This time, Gary Bentley had no doubt that he'd heard someone scream.

And it came right from the area I just left!

Without another thought, he spun around and ran back that way.

"Help me! Help!"

The voice was a little kid's. Gary ran even faster.

He reached the place where he'd earlier turned back. The growth of leaves facing him still seemed almost impenetrable, but he forced his way through and, a short while later, stepped through into a clearing.

Oh crap! he thought, on taking in the three corpses, one of which he immediately recognized as belonging to Slim Mitchell.

And Slim was with the kid and I just heard a kid screaming!

Gary looked around. "Jimmy, where are you!?" he shouted.

"Help, Uncle Ranger! Over here!"

Gary now saw little Jimmy Mitchell. About thirty yards away, the kid was climbing a tree. At the base of the tree, Jimmy's 'pet' was also trying to climb up after him, but was making hard work of it. The armadillo dug his claws deep into the tree bark and attempted to pull himself up the tree and then he repeatedly slid down again.

Gary cautiously walked towards Jimmy and the armadillo.

Yeah, I might've guessed. I was too damn late, and now there's another crackhead animal killing folks in these fine woods.

"Help, Uncle Ranger!" Jimmy screamed. "Rocky's gone crazy. He's killed Cousin Lisa and Uncle Slim, and now he wants to kill me too!"

"Okay, just keep climbing up the tree," Gary told the boy. "You'll be safe up there. Just stay there and wait for me to figure something out."

The only thing to do is to kill that damn armadillo, but how? It's so armor-plated now, it looks like it was built by the military!

And he needed to work out 'how' quickly because Rocky had just changed his tactics. Now he'd begun digging up the earth around the tree. Under normal circumstances, this would have been a long and arduous process that would likely have taken hours, worn the creature out, and given Gary sufficient time to call for backup.

But cracked up as Rocky was, the animal was digging around the tree like he was a motorized excavator. Gary was stunned by the speed at which a massive trench appeared around Jimmy's tree, with Rocky flinging loose earth out like his forepaws were sets of shovels.

I'd better get this done quick, before—!

"Uncle Ranger, Rocky is shaking the tree!"

And it was true. Now that the tree's roots were a bit looser, Rocky was slamming his body against it. Whump! And the tree leaned one way. Whump! again, and the tree leaned the other way.

Jimmy was holding on for dear life. But since he hadn't fallen out of the tree during the assault against it, Rocky once more busied himself with attempting to uproot it.

The tree's roots shredded, the tree shook, and Jimmy howled in terror.

And then Gary Bentley remembered the two chunks of Agent Orange in his pocket and he smiled.

The damn armadillo's having withdrawal symptoms. That's why it's so mad. It's so crazed now, it doesn't even know what it's doing anymore. It's so locked into its cycle of withdrawal-rage that it can't even smell the Agent Orange I have on me.

Gary quickly got the two chunks of Agent Orange out of his pocket. "Hey, Rocky, do you want these?"

And just like that, the atmosphere in that forest glade changed.

And just in time, too. Rocky had just rammed himself against the tree trunk again, this time succeeding in knocking the tree sideways to a forty-five-degree angle. This would have permitted Jimmy to climb higher into the tree, but would also have permitted the armadillo to easily climb up after him.

But now, as Gary brandished the two orange nuggets at the armadillo, he calmed. Rocky's ravaging mind recognized what the man across from him was holding as something desirable. Something he couldn't afford to miss.

Gary watched as the armadillo climbed out of the trench he'd dug around Jimmy's tree and started walking towards him instead.

Alright, Gary, you only get one shot at this. You gotta shoot that thing where it'll hurt the most. At least where it can hurt. It's lost an eye already. Maybe the pain it's in even prevented it from smelling the Agent Orange on me.

When Rocky was about five yards from him, and looked about to charge, Gary flung the pieces of Agent Orange over to the creature's right. As expected, Rocky instantly changed course to intercept them.

Gary hurried along beside Rocky. He'd figured out how to kill it now. It was simple, really.

With one eye gone, Rocky is blind on the left side. He can't see me coming. I just have to time my shot right.

And that's exactly what Gary did. While Rocky the armadillo scrambled in the grass to retrieve the precious drug, Gary positioned his shotgun right over its blind eye and pulled the trigger. He did this very carefully. Shotguns carried loads of pellets, and he didn't want to get ricochet-shot like Slim Mitchell had been . . . by this same armadillo.

So, Gary pulled the trigger and there was a loud explosion. Afterward, after noticing that Rocky no longer had a head, Gary Bentley walked over to the leaning tree and helped young Jimmy Bentley climb down.

"Thanks, Uncle Ranger," Jimmy said. Then he looked over at his dead pet. "Uncle Ranger, what made Rocky go bad like that and start killing people?"

Gary frowned and looked for words that a little boy would understand. "Kid, Rocky got some bad medicine, that's all. And the medicine made him sick instead of well . . ."

"Really, Uncle Ranger?"

"Yeah, Jimmy. You see, kid, some bad people make bad medicine that makes people sick instead of well, and you gotta be wary of those kinds of people, 'cos they don't care if they hurt you or not. All they care about is making money from selling their bad medicine to you."

"Really, Uncle Ranger?"

"Really, Jimmy. Now let's hurry over to the parking lot so I can call for the cops to come take away your uncle and cousin, and that other lady. And once that's done, we'll go off looking for your Dad and his girlfriend."

"I don't understand, Uncle Ranger."

"What don't you understand, kid?"

"I don't understand why anyone would wanna make medicine that makes you sick instead of well."

"Trust me, kid, I don't really understand it either. Some folks are just nuts . . ."

The End.

ABOUT THE AUTHOR

Gary Lee Vincent was born in Clarksburg, West Virginia, and is an accomplished author, musician, actor, producer, director, and entrepreneur. In 2010, his horror novel *Darkened Hills* was selected as 2010 Book of the Year winner by *Foreword Reviews Magazine* and became the pilot novel for *DARKENED - THE WEST VIRGINIA VAMPIRE SERIES*, which encompasses the novels *Darkened Hills, Darkened Hollows, Darkened Waters, Darkened Souls, Darkened Minds* and *Darkened Destinies*.

He has also authored the bizarro thriller *Passageway,* a tribute to H.P. Lovecraft, *When the Bedposts Shake*, an erotic horror, *THE BLACK CIRCLE CHRONICLES,* a five-part mini-series that includes the books *Prove Your Love, Strange New Powers, Night Wings, Sheep Amongst Wolves,* and *Lord of the Birds,* and the *CRACKIMALS* series of horror-comedies (featuring titles *Crackcoon, Crackodile, Cracksquatch, Crackroaches, Crackadillo,* and *Crackaroo*) in association with Director Brad Twigg and screenwriter Todd Martin of Fuzzy Monkey Films, who is doing their film counterparts.

Gary co-authored the novel *Belly Timber* with John Russo, Solon Tsangaras, Dustin Kay, and Ken Wallace, and co-authored the novel *Attack of the Melonheads* with Bob Gray and Solon Tsangaras.

As an actor, Gary has appeared in over a hundred feature films, including *Prove Your Love, Faded Memories, Midnight,* and *My Uncle John is a Zombie,* and multiple television series, including *House of Cards, Mindhunter, The Walking Dead,* and *Stranger Things.* You can also find Gary in the motion picture adaptation of *Crackcoon,* playing Jonathan, the forest ranger.

As a director, Gary got his directorial debut with *A Promise to Astrid.* He has also directed the films *Desk Clerk, Dispatched, Midnight, Godsend, Strange Friends,* and *Shoulder Down: Road to Redemption.*

OTHER GREAT TITLES FROM

Burning Bulb

PUBLISHING

WWW.BURNINGBULBPUBLISHING.COM

"Lots of action!" — Kimberly Bennett
Author, *Twisted Delights*

GARY LEE VINCENT

PASSAGEWAY

"This is a book that will keep you intrigued to the very end!"
—Christine Soltis, Author *Final Moon*

IMPOUND

GARY LEE VINCENT

GARY LEE VINCENT'S
DARKENED
THE WEST VIRGINIA VAMPIRE SERIES

DARKENED HILLS

When evil descends on a small West Virginia town, who will survive?

Jonathan did not start out his life to become a rambler, it just worked out that way. William was a troubled youth with something to hide. Both were from Melas, a small town tucked away in the West Virginia hills... a town where disappearances are happening more and more frequently.

After the suicide of a wanted serial killer, the townsfolk thought the nightmare was over. But when a centuries-old vampire is discovered they find out the hard way it's just getting started. Dark secrets can only stay hidden for so long and when the devil comes to collect, there will be hell to pay. Can Jonathan and William find a way to stop the vampire before it's too late? Find out in *Darkened Hills*!

DARKENED HOLLOWS

In the heart-stopping sequel to the award-winning *Darkened Hills*, Jonathan and William must return to West Virginia to face possible criminal charges stemming from their last visit to the damned town of Melas, where both had narrowly escaped the clutches of a vampire seethe.

And as livestock start mysteriously getting murdered with all of their blood drained, worried farmers are searching for answers - leaving the local Sheriff and his deputy racing against time to learn the cause before a more violent crime is committed.

Burning Bulb

WWW.DARKENEDHILLS.COM

GARY LEE VINCENT'S
DARKENED
THE WEST VIRGINIA VAMPIRE SERIES

DARKENED WATERS

When the world goes to hell, the chosen must arise!

As Talman Cane orchestrates a flood of epic proportions in this third installment of the *Darkened* series the towns of Melas and Tarklin are caught completely off guard by the deluge. Hell-bent on finishing what they started, the evil brothers return to the lunatic asylum to take care of the witnesses and add to the ever-growing army of the undead.

Aided by Lucifer himself and the insane vampire demon Legion, the stage is set to channel all of the forces of hell to come forth. In an all-out race to survive, Jonathan, William, and Amanda soon discover they are up against impossible odds as Lucifer opens the Gateway to Hell, ushering in the zombie apocalypse and the End Times.

Find out who will survive this cosmic battle of the ages in *Darkened Waters!*

DARKENED SOULS

Melas and the Madison House are about to be rebuilt.
True evil is about to be reborne!

Young ex-priest and vampire-killer William is drawn back to the West Virginian town that almost killed him, where his vampire arch-enemy Victor Rothenstein still stalks the earth.

The town of Melas lies destroyed after the battle of the End of Days. But why is wealthy Jackie Nixon so eager to rebuild it using the bone dust of murdered souls?

Terrible evil has visited before, but the Gateway to Hell is about to be reopened in a horrific climax. And this time – it's personal.

WWW.DARKENEDHILLS.COM

Burning Bulb
PUBLISHING

GARY LEE VINCENT'S

DARKENED

THE WEST VIRGINIA VAMPIRE SERIES

DARKENED MINDS

Jackie Nixon intends to become Vampire Queen, but at what blood-drenched cost?

In this continuation to the explosive infernal saga begun in Darkened Souls, newly-turned vampire Jackie Nixon is taking no prisoners. Accompanied by her daughter, Kate, and by the captive vampire lord Victor Rothenstein, Jackie Nixon explores the Darkness. There, she intends to rouse the slumbering vampire race, bound under an ancient curse, and with their help, rule the human world.

But there's a deadly threat to Jackie's plans. Not just William who is trying to stop her, but her own royal ambitions. If Jackie performs the ritual to wake the sleeping vampires the wrong way, she could instead free the Red Beast of Hell, an unspeakable evil that even the undead fear.

DARKENED DESTINIES

With over 45 people missing after Jackie Nixon's party, the mysteries surrounding Melas and the Madison House keep getting darker.

Now, with legions of vampires at her command, can anything or anyone stop her from gaining complete control over all mankind?

The final battle has begun! As the Vampire Queen ascends her throne and sets to unleash the full forces of darkness, the fate of all things good hangs in the balance.

Burning Bulb

WWW.DARKENEDHILLS.COM

WHEN THE BEDPOSTS SHAKE

An Erotic Terror

GARY LEE VINCENT

STRANGE FRIENDS

GARY LEE VINCENT

PROVE YOUR LOVE

GARY LEE VINCENT

STRANGE NEW
POWERS

THE BLACK CIRCLE CHRONICLES - BOOK 2

GARY LEE VINCENT

NIGHT
WINGS

THE BLACK CIRCLE CHRONICLES - BOOK 3

GARY LEE VINCENT

SHEEP AMONGST
WOLVES

THE BLACK CIRCLE CHRONICLES - BOOK 4

GARY LEE VINCENT

LORD OF THE
BIRDS

THE BLACK CIRCLE CHRONICLES - BOOK 5

GARY LEE VINCENT

From the Creator of DARKENED HILLS...

RIVER
A VAMPIRE'S NIGHTMARE

GARY LEE VINCENT

A Vampire's Nightmare Continues . . .

RIVER

BOOK **2** ICARUS

GARY LEE VINCENT

JEROME

A GHOST STORY

GARY LEE VINCENT

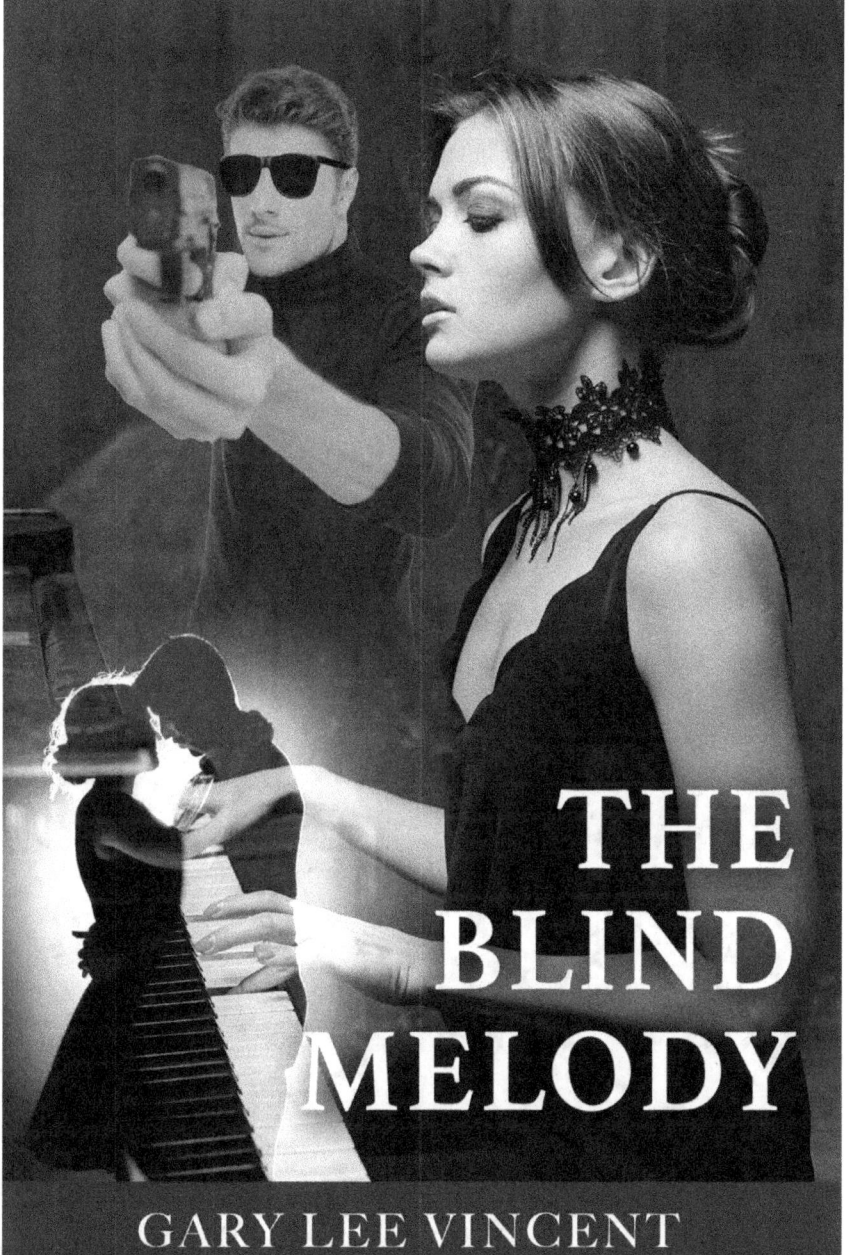

THE
BLIND
MELODY

GARY LEE VINCENT

RISE OF THE DEAD

AN EARTH-SHATTERING ANTHOLOGY OF ZOMBIE TERROR

Featuring Stories By:

John A. Russo   Tyson Blue   E.L. Stice   Nelson W. Pyles

Andy Rausch   Stephen Spignesi   R.D. Riley   Zakary McGaha

David J. Fairhead   Gary Lee Vincent   David C. Hayes   Rachel Montgomery

Paul Victor Wargelin   David F. Walker   William Vitka

Rich Bottles Jr.   Douglas Brode

Also, check out CRACKCOON, the motion picture from
Director Brad Twigg -- www.CrackcoonFilm.com

www.ingramcontent.com/pod-product-compliance
Lightning Source LLC
Chambersburg PA
CBHW070939250626
47159CB00009B/3311